THE
TOUCH

RANDALL
WALLACE

TYNDALE HOUSE PUBLISHERS, INC.
CAROL STREAM, ILLINOIS

Visit Tyndale online at www.tyndale.com.

TYNDALE and Tyndale's quill logo are registered trademarks of Tyndale House Publishers, Inc.

The Touch

Designed by Stephen Vosloo

This novel is a work of fiction. Names, characters, places, and incidents either are the product of the author's imagination or are used fictitiously. Any resemblance to actual events, locales, organizations, or persons living or dead is entirely coincidental and beyond the intent of either the author or the publisher.

Library of Congress Cataloging-in-Publication Data

Wallace, Randall.
  The touch / Randall Wallace.
    p. cm.
  ISBN 978-1-4143-4366-2
1. Surgeons—Fiction. 2. Grief—Fiction. 3. Biomedical engineering—Fiction.
I. Title.
  PS3623.A4438T68 2011
  813'.6—dc22   2011020427

US $14.99
51499

9 781414 343662   EAN

Printed in the United States of America

17   16   15   14   13   12   11
 7   6   5   4   3   2   1

THE

HOPE

1

WHEN MICHELANGELO FINISHED PAINTING the Sistine Chapel, neither the Pope who hired him nor the glorified artists of Rome took particular notice of the depiction in the center of the ceiling, where God, whom Michelangelo had the audacity to depict as a Being resembling a human, stretches His divine hand toward the first man, Adam, who is lolling in beautiful yet limp perfection, awaiting The Touch that will bring him Life.

The rich, the sophisticated, the high born, and the well-bred appraised the Chapel in numerous private viewings and judged it to be good work, perhaps even worthy of praise. They thought Michelangelo had displayed craft in handling the difficult curves of the ceiling and the added challenge of painting plaster while it was still drying. They critiqued individual figures throughout the fresco, but no particular section stood out in their notice.

It was not until they opened the Chapel to the hungry eyes of commoners, who would lock on those two fingertips, one Divine and one human, with Life about to leap, that anyone within the Vatican or the learned societies of Rome began to realize that The Touch was something special.

Faith Thomas and Andrew Jones were two of those commoners, among the centuries of tourists who had lifted their gazes within the Sistine Chapel to find themselves transfixed, open-mouthed, filled with wonder and joy. Faith and Jones, as she called him, were not in most ways what anybody would call typical; both in their midtwenties, they were an attractive couple, Faith with blue eyes and dark chestnut hair, and Jones tall and sandy haired, his eyes green and fierce. Among the tens of thousands of young Americans backpacking through Europe in the summer they stood out and drew as many glances as the statues and inlaid floors of the palaces they visited.

Still they were common. Both were from Appalachia, she from the coal fields of Pennsylvania and he from the Blue Ridge in Virginia. They had met in medical school. Now they were lying on their backs on the floor of the great Chapel, gazing upward, necks resting on their backpacks, each containing a battered copy of *Europe from $85 a Day*. Faith was worried the Vatican guards were going to tell them to get up, that lying in the middle of the Sistine Chapel's floor was not allowed on tour days or on any other days either, but Jones had whispered something to one of them when they walked in, and the guards seemed to ignore them after that. Maybe because it was the last group allowed in before the Vatican tours closed for the day.

The other tourists in their group had already gazed at the ceiling; their eyes already wore the glaze that comes from trying to capture and comprehend the greatness of a work of art whose subject, as well as the technique in depicting it, were beyond understanding. "The Divine Touch" was something to ponder; every person who lifted eyes toward it knew that looking at it was a privilege. But Faith Thomas and Andrew Jones lay on their backs below it and felt the thrill of a special privilege. To lie on a floor where thousands, even millions, of feet walked could have seemed unsanitary to their American minds, but the sanctity of the place made even the floor feel pristine.

"Is it the gift of life?" Jones wondered aloud to Faith, as his eyes, in sync with hers, drifted from the fingertips about to touch to the form of Eve depicted in God's other hand as a partner created for Adam. "Or the gift of love?"

"Both," she whispered back. "It says love and life are the same thing." Without moving her eyes for a long moment, she added, "You've got hands like that."

"Like Adam? Or like Michelangelo?" He was grinning; she knew the cocking grin without turning to look at it.

"Like the Big Guy with the white hair. Your touch brings me to Life."

In duplication of the painting he stretched his hand towards her; she extended her hand to him. But then instead of brushing fingertips, he surprised her by gripping her hand and pulling something from the coin pocket of his jeans and slipping it onto her ring finger.

It was an engagement band.

She rolled onto her side, looked at her finger, then at him. Suddenly they were kissing, and the whole room full of tourists was applauding them, and the guards were winking at Jones.

Even the painting directly above them seemed to glow brighter.

+ + +

There was no question in Faith's mind, of course, that she would remember that moment in the Sistine Chapel for the rest of her life, even if that life should last another hundred years, even if she should live long enough that she would sit drooling and could no longer remember her own name, the glow of what had just happened would nestle somewhere with her heart. As she and Jones walked hand in hand through the Vatican gates, she told him so.

He smiled, softly, and his eyes were bright with emotion, and though she had thought she could never love anyone more than she had loved him when he slipped the ring onto her finger, she loved him even more now than she had loved him ten minutes before. "You had all of this planned!" she said. "How long have you known you were going to do this?"

"Since I asked you if you wanted to backpack through Europe with me."

"I . . . I could've said no. I could've . . . I could've been too busy to come, I—"

"No, you couldn't," he broke in. "I wouldn't have let you."

She squeezed his hand and hugged her head against his shoulder as they strolled together through the warm and crowded streets, still filled with the sunlight of summer. Their hotel was two miles away, but they loved walking and would find a place to stop for dinner, a small restaurant with candles on the tables and singing from the streets outside. Faith adored the way Italians sang as naturally as they breathed.

Then another thought hit her. "Did you have that arranged? With the guard?"

"Sort of. Luca knew him."

Luca was an Italian friend they'd first met back in Virginia when he had come over from Rome to give a lecture called *Art and the Voice of God*. They had taken Luca to dinner after his lecture and the three of them had become fast friends; now Luca was waiting for them at a restaurant to surprise Faith again with a dinner to celebrate the engagement that Jones had planned. Luca would be bringing friends, none of whom Faith or Jones had ever met; but Luca promised that in an instant they would all feel like family, they would be family. Love did that, made families where before only strangers had been.

+ + +

Four months later, in the middle of a Virginia autumn, the two of them were driving into the mountains, a postcard of The Divine Touch taped to the dashboard of Drew's old jeep. Faith was at the wheel; after days in classrooms and clinics and twenty-four-hour shifts in Emergency Rooms she was always eager to feel the sway and the bounce of the road into the Blue Ridge, jostling up through the worn-out seats and humming through the steering column into the palms of her hands. That she felt such things, was aware of them, relished in the connection they gave her to the physical world, made Andrew surrender the wheel, though he enjoyed driving, just not as much as she did. He would watch her as she drove, and he would smile and shake his head and think of how lucky he was.

They had left the University in late afternoon and had taken 29-South into Nelson County, Virginia's poorest region. The road, however, was one of the most beautiful drives in the state, rolling and winding through farmland where houses and churches and stores selling antiques sat on ground that Thomas Jefferson had ridden past two hundred years before, on his way from Charlottesville down to Lynchburg to visit the summer house he had built there in a place called Poplar Forest. Jones loved history, so each time they drove this road he thought of Jefferson, the relentless builder, who designed Monticello and the University of Virginia and clocks and silver cups and—not coincidentally—was a designer of the United States. Faith would smile patiently as Jones reflected aloud about such things; she found them mildly interesting but rather curious, for Faith was much more interested in what was *now*, in those houses they passed where the Christmas lights would be still up in May or in October, and in the families who lived in them. Was someone sick? Why would they not take the lights down, so that putting them up again would be special? Faith and Andrew were two different people—and life between them was richer for those differences.

They turned west just as the sun went down beyond the ridgeline and the gray fog of evening had begun to bathe the forest and rise from the road in wisps. Andrew was on his cell phone; he didn't like to talk when they were in the jeep—their time together, away from the hospital, was too rare, and it was hard to hear in the jeep, but Luca had just called him and cell reception was spotty, so he answered, though his habit when traveling into the mountains with Faith was to turn his phone off altogether.

"Yeah, we're back!" he called over the noise of the snow tires singing over the blacktop. ". . . Faith? She's great! She's been strutting around in front of all the women in Charlottesville, bragging about how she captured me!"

Faith punched his shoulder, then reached down and took his hand. He squeezed it and said loudly into the phone, "We miss you already, Luca! . . . Of course you're invited to the wedding, I'll call you as soon as we set the date! . . . Sure, I'll give her a kiss for you! And she sends her love to you!" He hung up and smiled at her. "He says I should ask you about the project you were talking with him about while we were there, on the neurological effects of music."

"Early studies are suggesting that playing classical music to kids makes their IQ scores go up. It started me thinking: if music impacts the brain—"

"Post-traumatic coma. It might help induce healing!"

"Bingo, big guy! See, I knew you weren't just another pretty face."

"Why does it work? Soothing? Stimulating? Or that people get healthier when they're exposed to beauty?" He looked from the Michelangelo postcard on the dashboard to Faith's face. She had just switched on the headlights and they threw back soft reflections onto her skin.

"It's love. Art is an expression of devotion, a tangible proof that someone cared enough to make and share beauty. It may be that we doctors accomplish more just by the physical touching of patients, by showing them concern, than with our science."

"Love heals?"

"Love heals."

"Faith is the right name for you."

She smiled at him; then her eyes flicked back to the road and filled with terror. She jerked the wheel and opened her mouth as if to scream. But there was no time even for that.

In an instant, everything changed for Andrew Jones— all that he hoped and thought, all that he believed of life.

In an instant, Faith was gone.

2

WHEN LUCA HAD COME TO VIRGINIA from Rome to give his lecture on art and its interplay with religious belief, Faith and Jones had been undergraduates. Faith had told Jones she studied art to see naked men; Jones had said he liked to investigate the use of color. Jones claimed the truth was that he wanted to see pictures of naked women and Faith liked to investigate the interplay between what people believed as their spiritual doctrines and what they found beautiful.

So they had gone to the lectures of the young Italian genius they had heard about, this man who could lecture without notes and answer any question and talk for hours about art and life and beauty.

They were not disappointed. Luca Manzi was small yet exuded power, both in his physical presence and in his aura of intelligence. But more than brain strength oozed from the man; he had a great heart and it showed in his eyes. His hair was Italian black, his eyes a deep brown, his face handsome and covered in a five o'clock shadow no matter what time of day it was. Faith and Jones had found his class in the main rotunda building and eased into chairs in the back of the room and listened enraptured as Luca paced in front of the fifty students gathered there and spoke about art history from the first cave paintings to modern movies, the pictures that moved and carried sound and narrative with them. The compact Italian could carry all of that in his head; he saw it all and so could point it out and teach it.

When it was over they had walked up and asked him to go to dinner with them. Luca accepted; his eyes lit up and he laughed and then he said yes, he had not eaten and he would like to try American food. Faith insisted, over Jones's objections, that they take him to an Italian place but on the way Faith and Jones began to argue. "He'd like to sample what we call Italian here!" she whispered to Jones as they walked along.

"Our Italian won't compare to his!" Jones whispered back. "Virginia Italian isn't Italian Italian!"

Luca laughed and said, "The lovers are arguing, like lovers do! I wish I could paint you both!"

"You don't paint?" Faith wondered.

"I can't even draw well," Luca said, his whole face lighting up as he smiled. "I teach art, I love art, I share art, but I cannot make it. I am fine with this. I did not make the world, either, and I love living, especially when I am with two young people who love each other so much as you two do, and who fight as if they don't love each other and who care about nothing so much as they care about what each other thinks."

Now Faith and Jones were both smiling as brightly as Luca was. "So where would you like to eat?" Jones asked.

"I like Chinese," Luca said. "Or a steak. Pizza I don't care for."

They all laughed again and found a steak house. And there they had one of the great conversations of their lives. Luca told them about his girlfriend, a young woman who sounded clearly brilliant and full of life; as he spoke of her, Luca's eyes lit up. Her mother was an art dealer, and her father had been a film producer in

Rome. When Faith asked if they were getting married, Luca shook his head sadly and said that she was too young but that he loved her more than any woman he'd ever known.

"So you're having drama, then," Jones said, and once more Luca's face exploded with a smile and laughter leapt from his lungs.

"Yes, I have drama!" he said, his hands flying around in the air as he spoke. "I love drama, all Italians do! We cannot live without it!"

"Is that why you love art?" Jones wondered. "Because it is dramatic?"

"Life is dramatic! The very fact that we are here is dramatic! We have been made to live, and to be alive is to be in the presence of God!"

Faith had always been curious about the nature of belief. Jones had never felt her trying to convince anyone else to believe what she did; in fact it had always seemed to him that she was trying to deepen her own beliefs and wanted to know what was in the hearts of others. *Believe*, she had always told Jones, is a stronger word than *know*. So when Luca, who had just lectured so lovingly on the interplay between art and faith, so boldly declared that to be alive was to be in the presence of God, Faith lit up. "What do you think of God?" she asked. "You are Catholic, right? So how do you see the path to faith? Is it through morality, through grace, through ritual? How do you see it?"

Luca laughed again. "I see it in many different ways, every moment of every day. I believe, I doubt; I laugh, I cry." He took a sip of wine, shook his head, got lost in thought and then said, "But it doesn't matter. I don't need to understand. Nobody does. There are only two things anyone must know: there is a God, and that God loves us. That is all we need to know."

At that moment, hearing those words and the way they were spoken, Andrew Jones felt joy. Not the kind of joy that makes a person weep, but the kind that makes one laugh. He felt happy, in love, affirmed in all he had hoped and dreamed. He looked at Faith and saw her smile radiating love to him, to the whole world. He glanced back at Luca and saw him grinning.

"I think," Faith said, standing, "that says everything that ever needs to be said. So I'm going to take this opportunity to go to the Ladies' Room!" She kissed Jones on the lips, then kissed Luca on the crown of his head full of lustrous black hair. Both men watched her walk away.

Luca's eyes, deep brown and playful as a Labrador puppy, darted to Jones. "You are a blessed man," the Italian said and lifted his wine glass in a toast.

"Yes. Yes, I am," Jones said quietly. He smiled again. "Women love you, Luca. They all light up when you're around, and Faith's already running through her whole list of friends for all the ones she wants to set you up with. Why aren't you married yet?"

Luca wiped his face top to bottom with the palm of his hand and shook his head with a great sigh. "Many times!" he said, throwing both hands into the air. "Many times I fall in love. But she is always too young for me, too old, too rich, too far away, too lost in her work, or I am too lost in mine. It is a disaster!"

To Jones it sounded as if Luca had said, "Eeet ees'a deeSAAAHster!" and he struggled not to smile—but he smiled anyway.

Luca smiled too. But then he studied Jones as he might look at a fresh painting from a young artist. "What did you do?" he asked. "How did you two make it work?"

Jones nodded at the sincerity of the question and pondered it a moment. "I didn't do anything," he said. "What I mean is, I wasn't trying. I didn't have to try. I mean, at first. Because she wasn't trying. You know how you meet someone and they seem attractive and you think you'd like somebody like that so you try to be nice and right for them and you hope the magic happens. But soon you're trying more and the magic is less."

Jones glanced toward the rear of the restaurant, where Faith was stepping from the doors leading to the restrooms. She had stopped to talk with one of the waitresses; apparently Faith had complimented her on her earrings, and the two of them were examining each other's jewelry and laughing and oohing like sisters. That was Faith's touch—she loved everybody, and everybody loved her. "At night, I stop sometimes and look up at the stars. Everybody does that, I guess, but the thoughts we have when we do it, they feel so much like ours alone. When I was getting to know Faith, she looked up at the stars one night and she said, 'It's as if God made the universe and was so excited about it He just scattered sparkles of joy into the sky.'"

"Wow," Luca said.

"Yes. Wow. And I would've never said that, but it expressed exactly the wonder and the joy I was feeling. I knew then she was the one I wanted. Always."

Faith made her way back to the table. "What are

you boys talking about?" she asked, her eyes bright with happiness.

"Nothing," Jones said.

"And everything," Luca added.

There is a God, and that God loves us. That is all we need to know. Jones had thought of those words a few times before Faith's death and almost every day afterwards. The words made him angry. The words made him sad. But he could not let go of them, not because he believed them, but because Faith did.

Jones needed to believe those words, though he did not realize how much or how soon he would need to believe them, and that they would mean, literally, everything.

3

BLAIR BIO-MEDICAL ENGINEERING owned its own high-rise building, surrounded by some of the finest real estate in Chicago. They were a relatively young company, compared to the other businesses headquartered nearby, but in their field they were one of the oldest, their founder having been a pioneer in the development of machines that would make impossible surgeries not only possible but practical.

From the outside the building looked unremarkable, a tower of glass and steel with enough stonework to give it the stateliness of a business based on heritage, like a bank or an insurance company. But inside the building, where the labs and engineering workrooms formed the true heart of the company, Blair Bio-Med was a dazzling dance of lights, crisscrossed by lasers, encircled by computer screens, even sparkling with arc welders as their design teams not only devised but built the original prototypes of their inventions.

Those research rooms occupied the upper-central core of the buildings, and they were the building's heart. And in the very core of the research center was Dr. Blair's Surgical Sciences Suite. Dr. Blair—not the old Dr. Blair, who had founded the company, for he had passed away several years ago, but the new Dr. Blair, who had inherited all of his talents and all of his drive to succeed, not to mention all of the company he had founded—worked in these rooms every day and most every night. Dr. Blair was brilliant, and Dr. Blair was driven. And Dr. Blair was a woman.

Everyone who worked at the company—and there were some brilliant people at Blair Bio-Med—knew who the boss was, and they understood she was the boss not because the legal documents of her father's will but because of the force of her own will and her ability to turn will into action. They watched every action she made, as they watched now, when she lifted her gloved hand and signaled for an experiment to begin.

Technicians in the control room, separated by a double wall of glass from the surgical research table where Dr. Blair stood, ran their fingers over banks of buttons that sent power into lasers, shooting micro-thin beams in precisely aimed crisscrosses, an intricate maze of intense light that seemed to scan every particle of air in the space around the doctor and the work in front of her. Monitors on the wall directly beyond the surgical table displayed data updated thousands of times per second.

A human hand—Dr. Blair's delicate, feminine hand, made ghostlike by a surgical glove—slipped liquidly into a precision sleeve that fit like a second skin, containing sensors that recorded every movement of her arm, wrist, knuckles, fingertips.

She flexed her fingers. The microscopic sensors imbedded in both the surgical glove and the matching sleeve, spewed data that flashed onto the monitor screens and poured onto the computer hard drives arranged to collect it.

The woman at the center of all this was Lara Blair. Lara, without a "u." Her mother, a poet, had seen the film *Doctor Zhivago,* featuring a character named Lara whose lover was both doctor and poet. The new Lara had lost her mother early and had become a doctor, like her father. Now she wore full surgical attire: gown, mask, cap, clear medical goggles. Her eyes were striking—deadly serious, intense.

"I'm ready," she said, the words puffing against her mask.

An unseen technician's reply came to her through a speaker. "We are go."

Droplets of sweat glistened around the sockets of Lara's eyes. What she was doing had the gravity of life and death. She lifted a probe with a chiseled, razor point. She pressed her face into a set of surgical magnifiers that mimicked her movements and brought microscopic vision to her eyes. Using both hands to steady the probe, she threaded it through the matrix of lasers . . . and moved it down . . . down . . .

Into a brain.

Except this brain wasn't living. It was remarkably lifelike and was in fact an exact replica of a human brain exposed by the removal of a disc of skull at the base of a spine, but there was no body connected to all of this, and no blood. The micro lasers were aimed into and through the matter—mostly polymers of various densities—that made up the replica brain.

Standing in the back of the control room, behind the

technicians riveted to their monitors, were a man and woman, both in business suits. The man was Malcolm; slender, gray-haired and handsome in his late fifties, he had been the elder Dr. Blair's best friend, and would have been Lara's godfather, had her father believed in God. The woman was Brenda, who, at thirty-five, was seven years Lara's senior. Brenda had held various titles throughout her career, whatever Malcolm concocted for the company's board of directors to justify her salary, but what Brenda actually did was to watch over Lara like the sister she had never had, to bring an empathetic female presence into her life, to find the ways to nurture and protect her that Malcolm might miss. Malcolm had felt helpless as the elder Dr. Blair had worked himself to death, and he was determined not to let that happen to Lara. Malcolm and Brenda stood looking through the laboratory's observation windows, and they knew the stakes of the surgical trial Lara was about to attempt. They could barely watch.

And of all the focused people in the Surgical Sciences Suite, Lara Blair was most intense of all, her eyes dead still, transfixed as she shifted her instruments in tiny movements, deeper and deeper into the replica brain.

Then Lara froze. She had reached the section of

the brain where she, and every other surgeon who had attempted such a procedure, had failed in all their attempts.

The technicians in the control room looked at each other.

Malcolm and Brenda held their breath; then they too looked at each other.

Still Lara did not move.

A technician's voice came softly through the speaker mounted beside the camera array above Lara's head. "Dr. Blair . . . ?"

"Yes!" she snapped, swift and tense. She took a deep, long breath and closed her eyes for a moment, struggling down through the layers of her consciousness to reach a state of transcendent poise. Since her last failed attempt she had spent endless hours studying meditation and yoga to mold her body, mind, and spirit into a unified, balanced whole. She focused on her lungs, and inwardly she chanted, *breathe . . . breathe . . . breathe . . .*

She opened her eyes . . . burned her attention through the microscopic lens . . . and moved the probe.

Alarms screamed.

Lights flashed.

The monitors flickered on and off, and all of it shouted FAILURE.

The shrieking and flashing were obnoxious. The technicians sagged back in their seats. Lara slid her arm from the sensor sleeve, raked off the cap and mask, and took another deep breath, this one a full sigh of frustration. The door to the observation booth opened, and Malcolm and Brenda appeared beside her. Lara glanced up and shared a frustrated shake of the head with them.

An aide in a sports coat moved quickly up to Malcolm and whispered in his ear, "Sir, one of our scouts just brought in something that you really have to see."

As Malcolm followed the aide out of the lab, Brenda looked down at the simulated body on the table with the penetrated skull and exposed brain. "Sorry, Roscoe. She's killed you again." Brenda wore her hair long, curly, and unkempt—she claimed the static electricity of brushing was bad for the brain—and now she shook her wild curls and made a face, bugging her eyes behind her round glasses.

Lara shot her a stiff look. But if it weren't for Brenda's laughter, turning one more failure into just another bump in the road, Lara didn't know how she'd keep going. Even with her encouragement, with Malcolm and all the others—the best in the world—around her, she felt defeat eating her hopes. For the first time in her life she had begun to feel despair.

+ + +

The conference room of Blair Bio-Medical Engineering, with the view of Lake Michigan outside the high-rise windows and the company logo carved in onyx on the back wall, suggested a company that had seldom known failure—an extremely lucrative company that hadn't lost the originality of its core business. Drawings of new bio-medical inventions lined the wall spaces; mock-ups of works-in-progress were handy on the cabinet behind Lara's chair as she took her place at the head of the table.

Gathered around the long polished mahogany surface in front of her were the company's lawyers, accountants, and media advisors. All of them wore suits; her engineers, researchers, and the physicians on her staff were the only ones who dressed casually in the Blair Bio-Med Building.

Lara still wore her medical gear, having just come from the operating simulator. Freed from the cap, mask, and goggles, she was elegant, her dark hair luxuriant and her blue eyes strikingly bright, and yet she had no self-consciousness of her appearance, as if beauty was something she had never had time to consider. She was still dwelling on the failure of their attempt, staring out the window as one of her techs began the post-experiment analysis. He was one of her younger techs, two years out of MIT; Lara's father had started the tradition of bringing new perspectives into old problems.

"The difficulty occurs in the turn around the cortex," the young tech said and paused because he had no idea where the real difficulty occurred; nobody did.

"And how many attempts have we made?" Edwards, from Accounting, asked him.

As the young tech began checking his file to be sure, Lara snapped the answer: "Fifteen."

"From the point of view of strict cost-effectiveness—"

"Retreat is not an option," Lara said in a voice that allowed no discussion.

"We'll reconstruct the event and reformulate the route," the young tech answered.

Lara dismissed him with a tiny nod. One of her Finance executives cleared his throat for some new business. "We've encountered a serious pricing issue. We spent four years and 12 million dollars to develop our heart shunt. We knew what we'd have to sell it for to make a profit. But Marketing has a problem—"

"It's not Marketing's problem," her Chief of Sales broke in. "It's the company's problem. The national magazines are touting a new study that suggests—"

"Suggests?" Finance shot back.

"We have to take it seriously! It suggests Hispanics have this condition at an occurrence rate five times the national average. For us to charge—"

"We're a business!"

"So we can't look like gougers!"

Lara stood and moved to the windows, still lost in thought as the arguing continued behind her. Only Malcolm and Brenda, in the whole company, believed they could succeed with the project that had failed again that morning. The rest of the executive board was content to let Lara amuse herself as long as she wished, as long as they could keep the profits rolling in from the company's past inventions.

"So we explain our costs," the Finance guy said.

"No matter how much truth we tell," the Chief of Sales argued, "it won't matter. The public is emotional. We've had record profits—"

"—that we've earned through medical breakthroughs!

Lara, obviously you're going to have to settle this. Lara . . . ? Lara."

She glanced toward her executives, then stared out the window again. To them it seemed she had heard nothing of what they had been discussing. Then she said, "We trust the doctors." Everyone at the table tried to catch up with her thinking, and they were still sitting there blinking when she added, "Most doctors in this country do work they never bill for. And they know which patients have insurance and which don't. For anyone who can't afford the device, we provide it free—through their doctor. We also make a donation from our charity budget to a victims' fund, and host a fund-raiser."

"We're off the hook," the Chief of Sales said. "We look great."

"And we make a profit," Finance agreed and whispered, "Why didn't we think of that?"

Sales whispered back, "Because we don't own the company."

A breathless, excited Malcolm appeared at the conference room door. "Lara!" he called. "You've got to see this!"

Lara immediately left the meeting and followed Malcolm down a long corridor of cubicles to the stairway—Malcolm hated elevators—and they headed down two flights to the lab, while Lara's assistant Juliet called from the upper landing, "You have a financials conference in five minutes!"

"And I need your approval on the new graphics for the AMA Journal!" pleaded the copywriter who was waiting outside the boardroom. Lara and Malcolm disappeared into The Egg—the lab floor, where their new projects hatched. Malcolm struggled to contain his excitement. "For the last two years we've been beating the bushes looking for exceptional degrees of micro-manual dexterity to help with the Roscoe project. One of our scouts came across something at an art museum."

"An art museum?"

"I know what you're thinking, our scouts shouldn't be wasting time looking at art, and I wish I could tell you it was part of our master plan to expand into unconventional areas to find unconventional talent, but the truth is, the guy was traveling around from one university hospital to another and kept being told time after time that the surgeon capable of the microscopic manipulations we're looking for just doesn't exist. So he took a break and walked into an art museum. And there they had an exhibition called 'The Grandeur of the Small.'"

"He just stumbled onto it?"

"Fell face first into it."

They stopped outside a windowed laboratory where several researchers worked. The activity inside was modern Bride of Frankenstein: high-tech instruments with an inventor's disarray. Malcolm couldn't explain further, he had to show her. He pushed open the airlock door and led her into a room bright with white enamel and chrome. His briefcase—Lara gave it to him on his birthday, the first year she took over the company after her father's death—was lying on one of the lab tables. The briefcase was the company's version of a safe; anything Malcolm put into it was not to be touched. Malcolm flipped open the brass latches and withdrew a protective box of polished chrome. He opened the box. It appeared to be empty.

Malcolm lifted a pair of tweezers, and used them to withdraw an almost invisible object and place it on the slide of a microscope station. The microscope there was capable of sweeping views of the object on the slide. Malcolm dialed in adjustments—he was both physician and engineer, as her father was—then stepped back; Lara moved to the microscope.

She looked through the eyepiece, stepped back, caught her breath, and looked again. What she saw through the eyepiece of the microscope was a sculpture of Abraham Lincoln standing instead of sitting at the Lincoln Memorial. When she stepped back again, her thoughts were racing. And Malcolm was grinning.

She wasn't. "Exactly how small is this?" she snapped.

"It would fit inside the eye of a needle," Malcolm answered. Still grinning.

Lara looked back into the eyepiece. To the naked eye the object Malcolm held in the cushioned tweezers was no larger than a period in pica type. In the eyepiece Lincoln was majestic, chiseled as if from granite. There was emotion on the face of the Lincoln sculpture. Even discounting the carving's super miniaturization, it was a work of art, portraying the noble President having risen to his feet as if in outrage at the world he saw now. "And it's handmade?" Lara marveled, not quite able to believe what she was seeing.

"Not just that," she heard Malcolm say beside her. "It's handmade . . . by a doctor."

She backed away from the eyepiece.

"Using surgical instruments," Malcolm added.

She dipped her head once again to the microscope's eyepiece, to take in the magnificence of the minuscule carving. "A man capable of making this . . ."

"That's right. Could do anything."

She straightened and faced Malcolm. "What's the catch? Why isn't he here already?"

"We're checking him out now. But it seems this doctor, this . . ." He glanced to the notes his scouts brought him. ". . . this Andrew Jones? He quit operating. He supervises and teaches now, but he hasn't cut in two years. We'll work up a profile on him. Judging from the artistry of his work, this young doctor is deeply thoughtful . . . sensitive . . . a delicate man . . ."

4

AT THE MOMENT when the people at Blair Bio-Med in Chicago were trying to divine his softer qualities, the Dr. Jones in question was on a rugby field on the campus of the University of Virginia. The sky was slate gray and blended with the ground, where the previous night's thin snow merged with the mud into a crusty sludge. Anyone out in this weather had to be crazy.

And the rugby players seemed just that, scrambling around and banging unpadded bodies in the bitter cold. From a vantage point outside the game, it looked like chaos; from inside the scrum it was, well, chaos—colliding shoulders, banging heads, swinging elbows. A kicking foot punched the ball high into the air; it tumbled through the stony sky and fell into the gnarly arms of a runner, who plunged only a few steps before his opponents dragged him to the ground and the players bunched together again in another scrum, a melee of grunting men, all bloody knees and knuckles.

The players had no real uniforms; they wore shirts of two basic colors, depending on which team they played for that day, and shorts of any color at all; mostly, that day, the dominant color was mud. None of them had particular team loyalty; when not enough players would show up on a particular day, enough guys would swap sides so they would field even numbers. They did this for fun.

They shoved each other for a few seconds, until one of them got his foot into the scrum deep enough to rake the ball back to his team's side, and as the ball tumbled out they scattered into formation, racing down the field shoveling lateral passes from player to player. An especially burly brute caught one of these passes and was charging down the sidelines when a blur—the thoughtful, sensitive, delicate Dr. Jones—streaked into him in a bone-banging collision. Heads bashed; the ball went flying. But nobody worried about the ball because of the impending fight; with several players spread around the ground like train cars in a railroad disaster, the runner's teammate yelled at Jones, "Hey, man, this ain't American football!"

Jones jumped to his feet, and said, too close to his face, "It's America, isn't it? You think this sport is for wimps?"

"Who you callin' wimp?!" one of the other players barked, jumping up and shoving Jones as well as two more players nearby, all of whom had come out to wear T-shirts and shorts in the icy mud for exactly this sort of thing.

"It was a clean hit!" Jones shouted, pushing back. As more players joined the melee Jones grabbed the arm of the burly guy he leveled and started to help him up when he saw the guy's head was split open.

"Hey, Jones," somebody said, "you're not supposed to tackle with your face."

"He does everything with his face!" somebody else said. "Just ask your girlfriend!" All the guys were laughing even as they were shoving.

Jones prodded the gash on the head of the guy he had hit. "Come on, let me see, let me see. Hey, bring me my bag, will ya?"

Three minutes later the muddy, bruised, bloody

ruggers were clustered at the edge of the field, grimac-
ing like six-year-old boys as they watched Jones sewing
closed the gash on the guy's forehead. "Don't worry,"
Jones said. "You'll be pretty as ever! Scissors."

The biggest, gnarliest guy responded quickly because
he was, in fact, a surgical assistant. He handed Jones the
scissors from his medical bag—the one he always brought
to the games because stitches on the field were as regular
as cold beer afterwards—and Jones clipped the stitches
and was returning the tools to his medical bag when he
saw his cell phone flashing as he had programmed it to
do when the hospital called him in an emergency.

+ + +

Still in his muddy uniform, Jones walked into the hospital and called to Nancy, the Emergency Room nurse,
"What's up?"

"We've got a newborn who's not breathing right, and
the new resident in the ER doesn't have any pediatric
experience."

With the hurried focus of emergency, Jones washed
his hands as she slipped a hospital gown over his rugby
clothes. Nancy was forty-five and had raised two daughters alone and was now raising two grandsons because

one of her daughters was in rehab; Nancy was a natural caregiver but was also so tough that the joke around the Emergency Room was that if Hitler had had Nancy we'd all be speaking German. When Jones had started doing shifts in the ER as a resident eight years ago, she had treated him in the same way a general might treat a private, as if he knew absolutely nothing. Sometimes she still treated him that way. But when Nancy was on duty, no one ever died due to neglect, or because of a misdiagnosis by a rookie doctor. Jones preferred her over all the other nurses. "Is that your blood?" she snapped at him.

"I don't think so."

Twenty seconds later he was examining the baby, a trembling, boney mass that resembled a fetal bird more than a human child. "Looks like poor prenatal nutrition," Jones told Nancy. "How's her mother's health?"

"We didn't get blood work on her," Nancy said. "The baby was born on the gurney in the ER last night, while you were sewing up the drunk. The mother walked in out of the snowstorm and didn't even have a coat. She walked out this morning."

"Her daughter's frail, but she's hanging on. If she sleeps, she just might turn the corner. I'll watch her."

Jones pulled up a chair and settled down into it. Nancy looked down at his muddy, bloody knees, and he covered them with the surgical robe. "Did you sleep any?" she demanded, folding her arms across her chest and staring at him over the close-work glasses resting on the end of her nose. "You worked the last shift, you—"

"I'll be okay. Thanks."

She pushed the glasses up to the bridge of her nose with one finger, as if pointing to the spot where she would like to put a bullet between his eyes, and she left him.

+ + +

Lara worked alone, hour after hour in the lab, poring over the video of the operation they did that day. She replayed the move she had made that set off all the alarms. She was stumped.

Her father had once told her that all of his best ideas had sprung from a strange and unpredictable interplay between disciplined persistence and spontaneous inspiration. One had never come without the other, in his experience. There had been moments, he said, when ideas would appear in his head while he was driving to work and listening to music on the radio, his mind drifting to wherever the song took him; in those moments it seemed to him that the idea had ricocheted indirectly into his brain. In those times he would run into his lab and work for endless hours, inspired by the insight that had just come to him. Other times he would work for days, feeling he was doing nothing more than beating his head against a problem like a fly bouncing against a pane of glass; when finally he gave up and went home to let himself rest—when he truly let himself find release from the effort—a new potential solution just seemed to ooze into him like the warmth of a hot shower. He used that analogy because, literally, he had come up with the idea of one of his most profitable inventions while he was standing with his head under the beating jets of a shower after he had run for an hour on a treadmill.

Her father never spoke of what he might consider the source of ideas. He was not religious, and Lara supposed—naturally, it seemed to her—that he believed such a question to be unanswerable, so he decided at some point in his life to waste no time on it. And yet he attacked other questions, mysteries that most others in his field believed could not be solved. He never expected Lara to be a surgeon, much less a researcher and inventor; when it became clear to him that she had both the talent and the determination to push forward in the same battle he was fighting, he taught her everything he knew, and part of that knowledge was the strategy for increasing knowledge. A cornerstone of that strategy was: *Never be afraid to ask questions. What if? What if? Always ask, What if?*

He was a wonderful man, her father. He was kind and he was generous and it broke his heart when her mother died and that, more than anything else, was what brought the tears to Lara's eyes on the lonely nights during holiday times, whenever she thought of the family she no longer had, and in fact had never really experienced. She controlled great sums of money, she owned vast quantities of brain power, a great deal of it between her own ears, and she had friends she trusted—only Malcolm and Brenda, only two; but she could rely on them absolutely, and that was no small thing.

But her father had seldom held her in his lap, or read to her at night, or taken her out under the stars to look up at the sky and wonder how all that brilliance got there, arrayed in the heavens of the sky and the heavens of the heart. Her mother had done that with her, so long ago now. Her mother had used that phrase: the heavens of the heart. But now her mother was gone.

And Lara was still stumped.

No one in the company outside of Malcolm and Brenda knew how profoundly personal her father's quest for discovery was, or that it was even more personal, if that was possible, for her. They were searching for ways to save lives; how could any work be more important than that?

And yet, Lara thought, if we spend our lives trying so hard to hold on to life that we never live, never really allow ourselves the chance to dance and sing, what is the value—the wisdom, the use, the purpose, the importance—of that?

Still she was stumped. She turned to the microscope, and looked through it; she saw the tiny, hand-carved statue. She shook her head, marveling at it. She heard someone moving up behind her and knew it was Malcolm.

"Lara—" She didn't turn around. "Maybe if you tried to rest," he said, "and come at it fresh tomorrow . . . ?"

"There is no tomorrow, Malcolm." Now she looked at him, and saw the sadness in his face. "Sorry. You're right. I'll walk you out."

Except for the security guards, Malcolm and Lara

were the last to leave. As they stepped out of the elevator into the garage, a limo rolled up for Lara. But she waved it off, and the driver pulled back to his slot beside the guard shack. "Aren't you going home?" Malcolm asked gently, pleading.

"I'll sleep here. I want to go over the replays again."

"Get some sleep! I had to tell your dad that all the time."

"Did he listen? Listen, the doctor who did that carving? I want a folder on him by 6 a.m."

"Whatever you say, boss. Are you sure you won't go home?"

"I am home." She watched Malcolm walk to his car, then stepped back into the elevator and rode back up to the top floor, where no one was left but her.

+ + +

The chair in the pediatric ward was metal and would not have been comfortable to most people, but the cast-off baby had fallen asleep, her monitors were all steady, and Jones was nodding off. As the first clouds of sleep seeped in upon him, he began to twitch and make the sharp low sounds of fear. Whatever he was dreaming, it was a nightmare. He began to moan . . .

The terror of his dream grew. He began to struggle against the paralysis, the helplessness, of his dream. He was trying to scream, when he jerked, waking suddenly. He looked around and found himself still in the pediatrics nursery, silent except for the tiny bodies clinging to life.

He rose from the metal chair, reached down and with his hand delicate as breath he touched the abandoned baby on the cheek. She still slept.

Jones walked into the ER and found it calm; the young doctor on duty was asleep on a cot, visible through the open door of one of the examining stalls. Nancy, at the night-duty desk, spotted Jones and asked, "How is she?"

"She's gonna live long enough to need a name. And a mother. She leave an address?"

Nancy fished in her records. "We got it between screams, while she was in labor. But it won't matter much, she's not coming back." She handed Jones a slip of paper with a name and address. At that moment the door opened and a guy in motorcycle riding clothes— or half of them because his jacket had been sanded from his body by sliding across pavement—came in, assisted by two cops, one of whom was the guy Jones had sewed up at the rugby game.

Jones waved to the cop, and as the nurses moved to show the new patient into an admitting stall, Jones tucked the address into his pocket and headed toward the door. On his way out he stopped to wake the young resident. "Hey, Maestro, it's show time."

The resident stood quickly; sleep was a half measure in an Emergency Room. "What's up?" he wondered.

"Looks to me like a guy went down on his Harley and lost about, oh, three thousand dollars worth of tattoos." The resident was smiling as Jones left.

Jones drove six blocks to an ATM and made a withdrawal. He used cash so that he left no trail.

He found a surplus store, one he had used before; its neon sign advertised "Open 24 Hours."

+ + +

He drove along the cold wet roads into a part of town where no one had a credit card and what cash they had went to milk, bread, drugs, or sex. The sleeting rain had driven everyone else off the streets. A few young men watched from doorways, ready to move out and broker transactions. Jones stopped outside a block of welfare housing, and checked the address in his pocket.

In the unit on the first floor, a fifteen-year-old girl

was sitting by the grimy window, but she wasn't looking out at the rain. She had sat there a long time, by the look of her. She was holding a cheap but old doll— a doll saved from her own childhood. Tears slid down her face like the rain on the window glass. There was no heat in the apartment; her breath showed in the air, and she cradled the doll as if to keep it warm—and in so doing, to keep herself from the cold.

She was surprised by the tinny *bong* of the doorbell ringer. It disturbed her; who would be ringing her bell at this hour? She moved to the door and peered cautiously through the peephole. She saw nothing. Carefully she unlocked the door and opened it enough to peer out, with the chain catching. Seeing no one, she unchained the door and opened it for a better look.

Leaning her head outside her doorway, she found the hallway clear in both directions. But at the foot of the door was a bag. She picked it up gingerly and took it inside, shutting the door and triple-locking it behind her.

She opened the bag and withdrew its contents. An insulated, rainproof coat unfurled in her arms. At first she couldn't comprehend it. What was this? Who left it? Was it a trick? It couldn't be for her; no one in her life had given her anything—even the doll that was her only treasure was something she had stolen from a store. But the coat was in a bag—at her door. And someone had rung her bell. Could it really be for her?

Four minutes later she was wearing the coat and looking into the mirror over her bathroom sink. The mirror was cracked, and the silver backing had flaked so that the image seemed clouded, but she could see herself—in the coat. It wasn't rich; it looked like military surplus. But it was new, full length and heavy. She put her hands into the pockets and stared at herself in the mirror, embraced by the warmth and the mystery.

Finding something in the pocket, she pulled her hand out, and discovered she was holding several hundred-dollar bills.

+ + +

Jones returned to the pediatric ward and tossed his coat onto the metal chair. He was still wearing his hospital gown. He looked down at the baby. She was still resting quietly.

He sat down in the chair again and fell sleep. This time he slept peacefully, without dreams.

5

LARA SAT STUDYING THE eight-by-ten black-and-white prints that Malcolm had ordered done, photographic enlargements of the tiny sculpture their scouts had discovered. She, Brenda, and Malcolm were leaning over around the coffee table in Lara's office, a spacious, elegant suite with an imposing desk of English oak; the office connected to a tiny bedroom where Lara slept most nights now. Malcolm had already seen the photo enlargements, so as she sat studying them, he sat studying her; he knew she had been in the lab all night—she still wore the lab coat and the caps they used to prevent hair from contaminating samples. Pink edges of sleeplessness rimmed her eyes, and her voice, when she had greeted him that morning, lacked the firm edge of determination she always showed the outer world. Malcolm had seen her father fray too, when he had come to understand that never in his lifetime would he solve the problem he had dedicated his life to overcoming.

Malcolm had been with Lara and her father on the night William Blair died. He had suffered from lung cancer. He had been a lifelong smoker—it was an irony that so many doctors who knew full well the destruction cigarettes could spread through the heart and lungs could still succumb to the habit—and despite many efforts to quit (once led by Malcolm, who had also smoked during college, and who offered to quit along with him; Malcolm had succeeded, but William went back to smoking after his wife died) had never been able to permanently shake the habit. When William lay in the hospital on what they all knew was the last night of his life, Malcolm whispered to him, "I wish we'd spent more time trying to beat cancer."

But William had smiled then—actually smiled, behind the mask of the ventilator that kept his chest rising and falling—and shook his head; then his eyes turned to Lara, sitting in the chair beside the bed, and Malcolm knew exactly what that look meant, and what he would do for his dying friend and for his living daughter, as long as he would live himself.

Now Lara, seeing this new evidence of stupendous dexterity, tossed off the remainder of her lab gear and paced her office. Lara possessed the trait—some might call the affliction—of believing that if anything needed accomplishing, she had to acquire skill for it personally. But before her were the signs of a skill beyond any she could achieve herself; she knew that already, after a young lifetime of trying. She had never seen anything like the manual skill or the subtle artistry that the carvings demonstrated. The photo blow-ups made it even more evident than microscopic views of the carvings did.

Malcolm had also brought a folding file. He extended it to her. "Turns out we already had a file on the guy. He first came to our attention as a resident when his teachers started using terms like 'virtuoso' about his surgical technique. But he passed on our interviews, told our recruiters he wanted to practice in Virginia. Ended up at the state university, near the town where he grew up."

Brenda, who had served Lara's father as executive secretary for a few years after his previous secretary had retired, had read the file already. Brenda never forgot the details of any document she ever read, but she had clearly taken a special interest in this subject. "He lives in an apartment alone, gets paid ninety-two thousand a year, and has turned down offers for four times that. Teaches surgical residents and does double shifts in the Emergency Room—for no extra pay."

Then Brenda held up a small leather-bound book. "We found this in his file too. He wrote poetry for the university literary publication, while he was a resident. Listen to this . . ." Brenda opened the book to a page she had marked—she had taken the book home with her the previous night to study it—and she read:

". . . If love were a city on a hill,
with turrets tall and banners small,
where a king would die for his queen's soft sigh,
I could build it.
If love were a journey,
across the rage of slashing seas,
or through a wilderness of trees,
or across time . . ."

Brenda paused, to clear her throat.

". . . or across time, without the promise
that one who starts will find the end
then I would take the first step now
though I know my heart
if it should break
will never mend."

There was a pregnant silence in the room, broken by Malcolm. "There's an early picture of him in—"

Brenda lurched for the folder but Lara had already found the picture in the file; she plucked it out before Brenda could get to it, and studied it—a young doctor, virile and handsome. "Hmm," Lara said.

Brenda snatched the picture from her fingers. Lara took the volume of poetry from Brenda's lap and thumbed through the pages. "And we don't know why he quit operating?"

"We're sending a recruiter—" Malcolm began.

"No," Lara said sharply. "Find out if Dr. Jones is available for a personal meeting."

"When?"

"I'll be there in an hour. Two at most."

Brenda said, "I'm going with you."

Lara pulled the picture away from her. "No, you're

not." Lara studied the picture again, and without taking her eyes from it, she said, "He has The Touch."

+ + +

Andrew Jones's earliest memories were of smothering. He was an infant when his parents discovered he was susceptible to asthma. He did not suffer from attacks when he was at his parent's house in town, but each time they drove deeper into the mountain country, to his grandmother's house where his mother had grown up, his lungs would close down and he would begin to wheeze; within a couple of hours his lungs could barely expand at all.

That situation, all by itself, was not painful; he could lie there and pant for hours, even days, on end, and as long as he kept sucking in the tiniest breaths of air he could survive. None of the medicines the doctors had could help him. They administered many tests for allergies in hopes they could find out what the source of the reaction was; the tests told them he was allergic to dust and to leaf mold, among many other things, and both were prevalent on the farm where his grandmother lived.

Maybe his parents didn't understand how awful it was for a boy who loved to run and laugh and climb trees and wrestle with his cousins to have to sit motionless; but the young Jones understood from the beginning that if he panicked, if he started fighting for a breath, if he sucked hard trying to open his sealed lungs, he would die. He understood that he had to sit, absolutely motionless.

His grandmother knew not only this but that the boy's mind was going, going, never stopping.

Once the attack fully hit him—and they always seemed worse at night—he could not lie down; that made the feeling of drowning all the stronger. So he sat up. And Grandmother sat up with him. She held him on her lap and he would stare into her eyes, the color of a clear sky, as she told him stories and sang to him. All night long. All night long. All night long.

When he grew, he was determined to be stronger. Back at his parents' home, when he wasn't having the attacks, he would lie on his back with a stack of encyclopedias on his chest, hoping he might strengthen his breathing muscles so that he could grow stronger than the attacks.

In the summers his parents traveled; his father was continually looking for more promising work, as the economy was perpetually poor in Appalachia, and his mother went with him because she battled back pain from a spinal deformation that might have been corrected when she was a girl, but doctors were as rare as speedboats in the mountains. So Andrew spent the warm months with Grandmother, and she would take him to tent revivals, where they sang hymns like "Nothing but the Blood of Jesus" and "He Leadeth Me" and "The Old Rugged Cross," his grandmother's favorite. She would weep whenever they came to the line, "'Til my burdens at last I lay down," and he would imagine it was either because she would never cry about any burden she bore, any other place except in church; or it was because the thought of dying meant, to her, the thought of reuniting with her husband, Jones's granddaddy Rufe, who had died the year he was born.

The encyclopedias didn't help his lungs, though maybe they helped his mind. But the attacks kept coming. And through them all, Jones had learned to sit very, very still.

6

BLAIR BIO-MEDICAL OWNED two corporate jets, down from the four the company used before Lara took formal control and partnered with Malcolm in a program of cost cutting. Some efficiency experts they had employed as consultants had told them that with the flow of information available from the Internet their executives and researchers didn't need to travel at all, but Lara's father had taught her that data was just one kind of information; there was the other kind that you sensed and felt, knowledge that you imagined, and the history of discovery was full of anecdotes of scientists whose great ideas came not from the scientific method but from something more human—or more divine. When the legendary apple bonked Newton on the head and he was struck with the notion of gravity, he was not in his laboratory. And Lara's father, while agnostic, was not a cynic.

So the company kept two of its jets, yet Lara had not been in either for over a year. She preached to her people the power of a lifestyle balanced by family and hobbies and play, but she had buried herself in work for months on end. Now, as the jet carried her south and she looked out over the tops of the clouds and the endless blue above them, she felt that somehow, in some way the scientific side of her mind could never explain, her life was opening up.

She was the only passenger. On her lap she held the volume of poetry that Malcolm brought her, written by the Dr. Jones she was flying now to meet. Lara's eyes shifted from the pristine white of the cloud tops to the words on the pages of the thin book she was holding, and she reread the passage:

If love were a journey,
across the rage of slashing seas,
or through a wilderness of trees,
or across time, without the promise
that one who starts will find the end

then I would take the first step now
though I know my heart
if it should break
will never mend.

Lara closed the book abruptly and shoved it into her bag, as if to remind herself that she must be objective, even ruthless. She turned to the magazines the lone flight attendant had spread out for her on the table beside her seat—journals of finance, research, business administration. But one cover caught her eye. It showed a couple walking away from the camera with their child dangling between them, from their outstretched hands. The picture was on the cover to announce a story on genetics. But Lara's eyes stared deep into that picture, at the form of the child, suspended in the air and moving toward a rising sun.

Lara snapped herself out of that reverie too and lifted a journal on "Exciting News in Alloys and Metallurgy."

+ + +

Down in Virginia, at an Emergency Room in Charlottesville, Dr. Andrew Jones was finishing stitching a four-inch gash in a truck driver's head. "Next time you hug your wife after five days on the road," Jones said, clipping the last suture, "make sure you don't smell like a waitress's perfume, okay?"

"Thanks, Doc," the teamster said, surprisingly sheepish for a man whose back was hairier than his head. "I'll remember that."

"I bet you will," Jones said, and both men laughed.

At that moment, at the main entrance of the University Hospital, Frank Willig was shaking hands with Lara Blair. Willig was the hospital's chief administrator, and in his efforts to keep UV at the leading edge of teaching hospitals, he had made many purchases from Blair Bio-Med. When he heard its owner was on her way, he was determined to be the first to greet her. "We're so pleased you'd visit us in person!" he said in a voice he considered quite musical—Willig loved to sing karaoke, though no one loved to hear him do it—as he led Lara down the polished main corridor. The sun had come out after several days of rain, and light was pouring through the skylights. "We use your company's equipment, of course," Willig intoned, "and the grants from your Foundation are—"

"You're sure Dr. Jones is around this morning?" she interrupted, more harsh than she had meant to sound. She was determined to stay focused on her goals, but instead of feeling ruthless and businesslike she felt herself strangely nervous and unbalanced.

Just then they heard a call over the hospital's sound system: "Dr. Jones, Code 6!"

As Lara's eyes flicked to Willig he told her, "That's our emergency code for the operating theater."

"Do you have an observation balcony?"

+ + +

The surgical nurses were waiting for him in the sterile room, and they held up a blue gown to cover the hospital scrubs Jones was already wearing when he banged through the door. He washed his hands quickly, popped them through the sleeves, and stretched his fingers so they could glove him; as they slid on the cap and mask he snapped to them, "Who's cutting?"

"Stafford," the head nurse shot back.

Jones had been running, but when he backed through the second door into an operating room full of tense young surgeons around a patient whose head was curtained off, he exuded an almost casual calm. He turned and seemed not to notice the panicked looks in the eyes of the surgical team, the only part of their faces visible between their caps and masks.

Twenty-seven feet above and behind the patient's curtained head, Lara Blair stood next to Willig, and from the moment she saw Jones enter she understood the leadership and the confidence he was spreading; she felt it even at this distance, separated by a double layer of soundproofing glass. The students around Jones had recognized the master.

The lead cutter, standing at the head of the patient whose brain was the object of the drama, shifted so that Jones could move in beside him. Jones's voice was smooth and even; Lara could hear it on the speaker at the base of the observation window: "Pulse and blood pressure?"

The anesthesiologist, whom Lara noticed was the most veteran of the surgical team below her, monitored the array of sensors attached to the patient's body. "Rising, 180 over 150," he reported, and Lara understood his unspoken warning: *Not yet critical, but it soon will be.*

Beside her, Willig dropped his voice into a smooth baritone that he hoped would sound not only professional but seductive, for he found Lara Blair intensely appealing; he rumbled to her, "They often call Dr. Jones in, if the patient presents unpredictably."

Lara kept her eyes on the operating theater below

her and thought about that phrase: *the patient presents unpredictably,* as if the person strapped to the operating table—the son or daughter of someone, husband or wife of someone, father or mother of someone— had somehow just up and decided to surprise the surgeons with a little extra challenge, what doctors called a "complication." And for them it was a complication, because they had to scratch their heads and ponder and do paperwork afterwards; the patiently simply died. Lara was used to hospital administrators talking to her as if she didn't understand the nuances of what went on in the practical life of hospitals; she was used to it but still it rankled.

She heard through the monitor speakers the voices from the operating theater below her as the surgeon told Jones, "It seemed straightforward. Then we found a second aneurism, hemorrhaging behind the first . . ." The young surgeon's voice was tense, fragile.

"One thing at a time," Jones said, as easily as he might describe a play in rugby or pickup basketball. "You can do this, Ben. Retractor!"

The nurse extended an instrument to Jones.

"Not to me, to Dr. Stafford," he said. "Put it in your left hand, Ben. . . . Your other left hand." As the surgeon shifted the instruments that had suddenly become so unfamiliar to his fingers, Jones peered through the surgical magnifiers trained at the brain open below them. Lara could not see Jones's eyes, but she noticed the sudden stillness of his body, as if he'd put himself into a trance. Stepping back from the magnifiers he said, gently and firmly, "Now look at the brain. See what is. And see what has to be."

Stafford, the surgeon, pressed his face to the eye ports. "The first artery . . ."

"Right, it has to be clamped. So do it. Right now."

Lara could tell Stafford's fingers were trembling, though it may not have been her eyes but her gut that told her so—just as she could tell that Jones's hand was perfectly steady as he gripped Stafford's wrist and moved it into position. Then Jones drew his own hand away. "Shift the artery clear, then clamp it," he ordered.

Stafford had frozen. He just could not get his hand to move.

Then Jones surprised everyone in the operating room and on the observation balcony, including Lara. He looked away from the patient, directly into the eyes of the frozen surgeon, and said, "Hey, Ben, you hear about those two drunks staggering home one night, when one of 'em says . . ." Jones leaned closer to the young surgeon and dropped his voice, so that no one outside the operating team could hear his voice again until he said, casually yet firmly, "Clamp it, Ben."

Stafford made a move and inserted a clamp.

"Good. Now the second artery!" Jones said clearly, and his voice dropped again and picked up the quiet narrative he had begun. Lara, Willig, and the others on the observation balcony strained to hear, but all they could catch were occasional words. Lara thought she heard him say, ". . . stinking drunks . . ." and ". . . the lady wouldn't open the door . . ." And Lara began to smile.

"What's he doing?" Willig wondered aloud beside her.

"He's telling a joke," Lara whispered. "Probably a bawdy one."

Down below her, Jones lifted his voice again, enough so that Stafford heard the next instruction without tensing. "Scalpel," Jones said, then dropped back into his easy narrative as Stafford began what Lara knew was an even more delicate maneuver inside the patient's brain. Jones's eyes flicked to catch every move the rookie surgeon made, yet Jones never broke stride in his narration.

And Lara never took her eyes from Jones, while Willig squirmed a bit next to her, no doubt uncomfortable about the apparent impropriety of a bawdy story during a life-and-death procedure. But Lara had the opposite reaction; she watched in reverent wonder. She had spent all of her professional life working at the limits of human ability; she carried within her the skepticism of the scientist, yet even deeper in her heart she harbored the secret hope of wanting to matter, to live, to save. She knew that doubt and hope were at war within the young surgeon, and that Jones was using all the tools of his own courage to distract the doubt and let the hope, the patient, and even the young surgeon blossom into life.

"Now listen, this is good!" Jones was saying. And he lowered his voice again until he said strongly, "Good. Clamp."

Stafford was nearly hyperventilating as he readied himself for the most crucial move inside the patient's brain. Jones watched his movements, knowing what was about to happen before it happened, while unrolling his story like a buddy at a ball game. All Lara could make out was the punch line: "He staggers off the porch and his buddy says, 'When did she say they open up again?' And the second drunk says, 'I think she said 'Thhhhhhhursday,' but her breath was so bad I didn't want her to repeat it!'"

Stafford made the cut; Jones handed him the second clamp and Stafford instantly inserted it into the brain. Jones and Stafford looked at the anesthesiologist, who checked his sensors and nodded. The patient's vital signs were all showing strength; the operation was a complete success.

Stafford stepped back from the table, relief flooding so fully from his heart that his legs buckled slightly. Then he looked at Jones. "Thhhhursday?!" Stafford exploded. And all the surgeons burst into laughter.

In the observation balcony, Willig was flushing with embarrassment.

Lara Blair was transfixed.

+ + +

Jones was a self-contained man who attended few of the formal functions of the medical school faculty and tended not to return phone calls pertaining to paperwork and bookkeeping, so a few years back the administration had provided him with a bright young secretary named Janet. Jones liked her and referred to her as his electronic dog collar. Janet's office—Jones refused to call it his own—was on the basement floor of the Med School, closest to the surgical center. As Jones entered and moved past Janet's desk in the outer office, she said, "Dr. Jones, you have a—"

"I know, I know, but I gotta have some breakfast, or—whoa, it's almost dinner time. I gotta get something to eat." He continued without stopping into his office, stripping off both the surgical gowns that covered his filthy T-shirt and bloody, muddy rugby shorts over his skinned-up knees. He was tossing the surgical gown onto the hook on the back of the door when he realized he was not alone in the office; a beautiful, elegantly dressed stranger—Lara—was sitting on the chair in the corner, waiting for him.

"Doctor Jones?" she asked, as if she weren't already sure it was he.

"Uh, no!" he sputtered. "Jones, he's uh . . ."

But before Jones could escape his embarrassment, Janet took delight in calling through the open doorway, "You have a visitor, *Dr. Jones!*"

"Thank you, Janet," he said sharply.

Janet almost sang it, in a soprano that would have matched Willig's baritone: "You're welcome, Dr. Jones!"

Lara had taken in every fragment of this exchange; her eyes were such a cold blue they added to the impression that her stare was frozen, but Jones had seen that

miss-nothing look only on the faces of the brightest people he had ever met; Lara's eyes reminded him of another
pair of eyes he tried never to think about. Lara rose easily
from her chair. "I'm Lara Blair. I'm with Blair Bio-Medical
Engineering. I'm sorry to barge in on you—I understood
you'd be available for a few minutes after your rounds."

"Uh . . . could I get you some coffee or anything?"
he asked.

"Your secretary already offered, thank you."

"Yes, she's very efficient," Jones said in a tone he
knew Janet would notice.

"Thank you, Dr. Jones!" Janet sang from her outer
office.

Jones shut the door and moved to his desk, he and
Lara studying each other, taking each other in. "Laura
Blair?"

"It's Lara, actually. But yes, Blair. My father started
the company."

"Your father is William Blair? He was a brilliant surgeon. I studied his techniques and learned on instruments he designed."

"He died four years ago and left me the Bio-Med
devices company, and also the Blair Foundation,
through which we fund surgical research."

Jones had dealt with many offers to work for development companies, and he sensed where this was leading. "I'm a teacher now."

"You're the best micro-manipulator we've ever seen. You may be the best anybody's ever seen." She opened her briefcase and lifted up the acrylic box containing the tiny sculpture Malcolm's scouts had brought her. "One of our scouts came across this a few days ago. Dr. Jones, I have degrees in medicine, engineering, and microsurgery. I'm as good as anyone in our company— probably better. But I can't do what you can do. I'm working on a device that would save lives—and make a lot of money. We need your skills."

Jones moved behind his desk, as if it were a wall. ". . . Well, I'm sorry for you to waste the trip, but—"

"Before you give me your answer, could I show you some scans?" She pulled a scan from her bag. Jones hesitated, then popped the scan onto the light-box on the wall behind his desk. The scan displayed the interior of a patient's brain, with light and dark areas that even many doctors could not have made sense of.

Jones sized up the scan in an instant. "A double aneurism. Clip one off, the other blows out. Finally somebody developed the simultaneous clipping technique. That, I believe, was your father, William Blair."

Lara handed him a second scan. Jones needed only a glance. "This is the fool's gold of brain surgery. The patient spends two hundred thousand dollars and six months of recovery on a procedure that gives 'em four more years of life—but they would've had five without the surgery because the procedure weakens the artery walls."

"My company's just developed a titanium shunt that reroutes the blood flow from the problem area so that the prognosis is, essentially, normal life."

"That's a great idea; who came up with that?"

"I did; what about this?" she said quickly, handing him another scan.

Jones took the translucent scan from her hand, slid it into his viewing box, and stared at it for a long moment. She drifted up beside him to study the scan—and his reaction. He was silent for a moment, almost reverent, before he spoke. "I've seen two of these in my whole career. The condition is congenital. It manifests like a tumor and confuses Radiology when they can't find one. The problem has to do with this artery here. It could be shunted off and made normal, except that getting to it requires passing through twisting canals of bone and artery, and then through this area that controls all brain function, and threading instruments through that region destroys the patient's brain."

Janet poked her head into the office. "They want you in the pediatric ICU," she said.

The next moment confirmed for Lara Blair her initial instinct about Jones: that nothing he did was casual, lacking the sharp edge of intensity. She watched him grab for his surgical gown, and she was already picking up her bag.

+ + +

Jones hurried down the hallway with big strides, wrestling back into his surgical gown as he went. Lara rushed to keep up, talking as they walked. "Could you work a needle probe into that area?" She knew he understood the area of the brain she was talking about, the one that no surgeon had ever penetrated without destroying the brain he was trying to save.

"Me? No," Jones said, never slowing.

"I mean someone with your skill, someone who possessed your ability. Could it be done?"

"Maybe," Jones said, still not looking at her. "But it wouldn't do much good."

"But if you—if anyone could get a probe into that area—"

"It's not just a probe; the thing has to be clipped. A tumor you can freeze, but an aneurism is a weak vein—"

"I know what an aneurism is."

"Then you know what you're talking about is impossible." They turned a corner and were almost to the door of the Pediatric Intensive Care Unit. Jones glanced at Lara, still following him, refusing to give up. "Nearly."

"You're hooked! Aren't you!"

Jones banged through the door of the pediatric unit, Lara right behind, then scrambling alongside him and arguing to answer his unspoken protests, her voice both insisting and excited. "Yes, you are. Yes, you are!" But she stopped talking as his eyes, bright with concern, darted to an empty incubator.

Jones looked to the pediatric nurse, concern, almost panic, registering on his face, but she was calm, almost but not quite smiling.

For a moment to Lara, whose every sense and every instinct were fully charged to read Andrew Jones, he seemed out of sync, the nurse's peace at odds with the sense of emergency that had driven him down the hallway. Then the nurse's eyes directed his attention to the other side of the room.

There a fifteen-year-old mother, cradled in a new coat, was holding her baby as before she had held the doll, and was staring down at her real child.

Jones moved to the nurse. Lara stayed back, but she could hear the nurse whisper to him, "She walked in here this morning and said she wanted to hold her baby. I thought it was something you'd want to see."

The baby emitted a feeble but healthy cry. The young mother looked up to the nurse, who had just warmed a bottle and now carried it over, showing the girl how to feed her baby.

Jones stood quite still and watched the girl tuck the bottle between the lips of her baby.

He looked at her in the same way he would look at sacred art, for though a mother feeding a newborn was something that happened millions of times a year throughout the world, there was something in this that was holy; Lara studied him, and she knew something out of the ordinary had happened there, though she could not have said what, she could not have known that something in this was even greater than what Jones had once seen at the Sistine Chapel, for this was alive, this was the Hand of God to Andrew Jones. But one can stare at the holy only for so long, and one cannot watch a fifteen-year-old mother for too long either, without making her feel uncomfortable. Jones glanced to Lara, and they moved back out into the corridor together, easily, as if they'd already found a bond.

"Look," she said, "I'm sorry to dog you about this. Last year, worldwide, 128 people died of the condition I showed you. In three years that's like a jumbo jet crash, and nobody else is working on the problem. We're perfecting a computer-mechanical interface, we've created a practice environment—we're so close! Just . . . before you say no, will you let me buy you dinner?"

She watched him, and the longer he hesitated, the better she felt.

"Can I take a shower first?" he asked.

Lara smiled—and it was the happiest smile that had played across her face since she was child, before she knew her mother was dying, before she knew anyone, anywhere, ever had to die at all.

7

LARA HAD ALREADY PICKED THE PLACE and made a reservation for a quiet table for two in the restaurant of the Jeffersonian Hotel, Charlottesville's finest. Starched white tablecloths and six wineglasses were already on the tables when she scouted the setup that afternoon, and she pointed out to the maitre d' an area close enough to the fireplace to be cozy and not so close as to feel intentionally romantic. Lara had spent every day of her business life threading the needle through an ever-narrowing space between drawing men close enough to negotiate and keeping them far enough away to remain professional.

She had also booked a room for herself in the Jeffersonian and had her flight crew staying at the much more modern hotel out near the airport; they were always prepared to take off within an hour if Lara's plans should change. Now her schedule was uncertain, but her plan was not: she was there to recruit Dr. Andrew Jones into her company, regardless of the effort, regardless of the cost, and her determination to succeed had grown with every minute she had been around him. She admired his focus, almost fierce in its intensity; yet he had a playful balance, and his grace under fire was downright inspiring. Her scouts had searched the world for a person who could do what she needed done, and here he was, just a short plane ride from Chicago—if only she could find a way to overcome whatever the demons were that had kept him from applying his great skill on living patients.

Lara was not prepared to take no for an answer. But there was something else she was not prepared for, and that was the effect Jones had on her secret self. Lara considered herself the ultimate pragmatist; she did not believe in a soul. She understood the word as a poetic concept, of course, a metaphor for the quiet and pleasant emotions she allowed herself to indulge in at the rarest of moments. She considered these lapses into peace and awe and a sense of being a part of something beyond the capacities of her intellect to be dangerous. Whenever she experienced such moments—a brush with unexpected beauty, a sense of a message of love coming to her when she heard no voice and believed in no Speaker—she accepted them absolutely, during the very moment when she felt them. But afterwards she always told herself she had felt nothing except her own longings, and those longings she considered pitiful at best and dangerous at worst. She tried to keep such longings—for connection, for union, for peace, and . . . yes, for love—out of her mind and out of her life. That's why they were her secret self.

Something about Jones spoke to that secret self. And while Lara had always been careful to keep men far enough from her own attractiveness so that she could do business with them, she now felt she must keep herself far enough from Jones so that she would not do something stupid and even potentially disastrous, something like falling in love.

So she showered and washed her hair and brushed it back simply and kept the makeup to a minimum and wore a navy blue jacket with slacks and low heels and only a strand of pearls, the ones her father had brought back to her from a trip to Japan, and she told herself she was dressed in a thoroughly businesslike way; but she did look at herself in the mirror for a long time, and used a fingernail to perfect the lipstick at the corner of her mouth, and brushed her hair again and checked herself in the full-length mirror beside the door of her room before she headed downstairs.

When she stepped into the lobby, Jones surprised her by being there already, standing by the windows, looking out into the night. As he saw her reflection he turned to her and smiled. He had showered too—his hair still looked a bit damp—and now sporting a coat and tie, he looked great. "Hi. I . . ." she began, and for the first time since they met, she seemed unsure what to say next. But indecision never lasted long with Lara; she told him, "We have a few minutes before our reservation and I've been sitting most of the day. Do you mind if we walk around the block before dinner?"

"Not at all," he said. "I could use some fresh air myself.

They turned to the door and bumped into each other as he moved to hold it open for her. They both laughed.

+ + +

The sharp cold of a cloudless November night in Virginia stung their faces and the air prickled as it filled their lungs; the temptation to turn right around and go back inside could have been strong, but both Lara and Jones were smiling as they breathed deep and took in the black sky blazing with billions of stars. Lara could not remember ever having seen so many, and silently she told herself, *Don't start doing that, Lara; don't be looking at the stars and thinking you've never seen them so bright.* They strolled along the sidewalk of Charlottesville's central street, and Lara said, "The Jeffersonian Hotel, Jefferson Restaurant, Jefferson Muffler-and-Mule Feed. . . . Does this town have a fetish?"

"Jefferson set the tone for Virginia with designs he built here. Monticello, the University . . ."

"Did you carve him too?"

"He's my favorite. 'I have sworn, upon the altar of God, eternal enmity—'"

She finished the quote: "'—against every form of tyranny over the mind of man.'"

He looked at her in surprise. She smiled.

"You like Virginia?" she asked.

"I love Virginia. Especially this part, the Piedmont, the 'foot of the mountains,' where the coastal plain collides with the Blue Ridge. Virginia has such rich history—the first permanent colony of Europeans landed at Jamestown in 1607; the Pilgrims in Massachusetts had better publicists, but Virginia was first. So many of the great men of America's past were Virginians—Jefferson, Washington, James Madison, Patrick Henry, Robert E. Lee, Stonewall Jackson—they were all Virginians. But it's the common people I really love, the ones that came over as indentured servants and pushed their way into those mountains when there were no roads, no towns, nothing to depend on except themselves and God, and they did it because they were determined to choose their own path and not be ruled by someone else." Jones paused, saw that she was listening eagerly, and went on. "During the Revolutionary War, when Washington was losing every battle, he said, 'If this war continues to go badly I will withdraw into the Blue Ridge Mountains and plant my flag among the Scots-Irish, who will not submit to tyranny as long as there is a man alive to pull a trigger.'"

Lara saw the energy alive in Jones, the passion burning so brightly that it seemed for a moment to blot out the stars. She watched him in fascination; she had never met any man like him. But the moment she realized that, another voice inside her told her to be careful; men, especially the ones who had intrigued her, had always disappointed her in the end.

Then she noticed that Jones had stopped as if he too had caught himself and was turning inward. Maybe he thought he was talking too much. Maybe he thought he was enjoying himself too much. Lara wasn't sure. "Please don't stop talking," she pleaded. "This is the first interesting conversation I've had in five years." As she said this she patted his shoulder and was surprised that it was hard as a bowling ball; most doctors, if they exercised at all, jogged or swam to keep their hearts healthy; Jones felt like a boxer.

Jones smiled—he seemed to Lara to be enjoying himself—but he did stop talking for a moment, and led her across the quiet street, and they strolled in the opposite direction, past more antique shops and hardware stores and small businesses that sold drapery and wallpaper. Then Lara looked up again and halted; one of the streetlamps was out, and in that deeper darkness the stars showed in even greater numbers. Jones gazed up too and said, "Yeah. That's another thing about Virginia: we have great stars, especially this time of year."

"I don't look at them enough," Lara said and immediately regretted it because she was being too personal, opening up too much. For two days she had been excited in anticipation of meeting him, excited for reasons that were anything but professional. Over and over she had reminded herself that this evening was all about Dr. Jones and getting him to do what she needed him to do.

But she kept having the feeling that he was isolated in his life as she was in hers, and as hungry to talk about the wonders that lay beyond the boundaries of work and career. As they strolled back toward the restaurant he said, "I heard something recently about the Hubble Telescope." He paused, as if unsure about letting the conversation wander.

"The Hubble? What about it?" Lara asked. "I'm like every girl; I love the stars."

"The director of the Hubble project, as one of the perks of being director, gets a little time each month to point the telescope anywhere he chooses. So one month he decided he wanted to explore a tiny piece of the cosmos that was totally black. I believe it was somewhere within the Big Dipper but I'm not sure; wherever it was, it had been the accepted wisdom of every astronomer in the world that there was nothing there. And his fellow scientists in the project all urged him not to waste his time, because they'd pointed many telescopes at that spot before, and they'd found nothing but black emptiness. But the director said he wanted to hold the Hubble on the spot and do a long time exposure and see what they came up with. And he was the director and it was his privilege so they did it. And they discovered that empty hole in the heavens had—are you listening?—*two thousand galaxies.* Not two thousand stars—two thousand galaxies! And get this: the size of the spot we're talking about is the area you'd cover if you took a grain of sand and held it at arm's length against the night sky. That small. Two thousand galaxies. Billions and billions of stars. That's how much our science had missed."

Jones paused again and thought of his grandmother. He could hear her voice, reading from the Bible she kept tucked along with the pistol in the table beside her bed: "*What is man, that Thou art mindful of him?*" He looked up, surveying the stars. "My grandmother loved the stars," he said quietly.

"Tell me about your grandmother," Lara asked.

"I don't know you well enough," Jones said. And they strolled back toward the restaurant.

+ + +

Lara knew they would have a nice table—she planned for good results, and expected them—but she was both surprised and delighted when the maitre d' showed them to a nook near a window looking out toward the mountains, blue in the light of the rising moon. As they settled into their chairs—Jones held hers for her, like a gentleman, and she thanked him, like a lady—she said, "When did you start writing poetry?"

"You know an awful lot about me."

"We have a lot at stake in whom we choose to work with. Not many doctors are literary, but those who are tend to be extraordinary."

"Chekhov said, 'Medicine is my wife and literature is my mistress. When I—'"

"'—When I grow tired of one, I spend time with the other.'"

"You know Russian writers too?"

Lara already knew that Jones was smart enough to see through any manipulation; she desperately needed to recruit him, but something about Jones made Lara want to be completely honest with him. "I know a few. And I have a good memory," she said. And then she confessed, "We found out that you love them, so I read up a little." She noticed the reaction in his eyes, the defensive withdrawal there, and she added, "I'm sorry. I see you feel we've been prying. But talent like yours is more than rare. So let me get this out of the way. I've come to offer you a million dollars. And I'll write the check tonight."

Jones was studying her, his gaze penetrating, his smile gone.

Lara went on, "We'll fund the development of any new instruments you might invent and give you half the proceeds from their sale. There are no strings attached—except that you pursue your surgical specialty." She stopped and let that sink in.

He was staring at the tablecloth between them, and now it seemed like a vast field of snow.

She leaned forward slightly, slowly, taking care to keep her voice even. "We're aware there is a complicating issue."

"And you know the issue."

"Only that it's personal. It has to be; you loved being a surgeon, as every true master loves his art. Whatever stopped you didn't take your ability, otherwise you couldn't be making sculptures with emotion and beauty and character, all small enough to fit inside the eye of a needle. You can do what we need done."

"I'm not a surgeon anymore," Jones said quietly. "Now I teach other doctors to operate."

"What about teaching them to do what no one else has ever done?"

Jones looked away, his eyes and his thoughts wandering across the distant mountains. Lara knew she had already pushed too hard, had already violated an internal space, perhaps a sacred one; but she could not give up. She added quickly, "I have a colleague—a friend—who works for my company. She's a psychologist, she's excellent. Maybe if you and she sat down together and talked about the issues that—"

Jones pushed back from the table, with icy calm.

Lara spoke hurriedly. "I'm sorry. I shouldn't have said that."

"No, it's fine."

"No, please, it's not fine."

"I'm sorry I've wasted your time, and I don't want to waste your dinner. It's been . . ." Without another word he stood and walked out.

+ + +

Jones was striding quickly along the sidewalk when Lara broke from the restaurant doors and rushed to catch him. "Dr. Jones! Please—I'm sorry! Your life is your life, and I don't mean to violate your privacy. I know I've done that already, it's just . . . this project means a lot to me, personally, and . . . I just don't know when to quit."

Without breaking stride, he said, "And you think maybe I'm a quitter?"

"I didn't say that!"

"No, I said that." Jones stopped and wheeled toward her, but instead of staring into her he stared away, some argument raging within his own head. She watched him, and she did not push him now; she had pushed too much already.

And in that moment an awareness dawned in Lara that both thrilled and disturbed her; she realized that Jones found her as unique as she found him. She knew he wanted to walk away from her and her offer the way he had walked away from everyone else who sought to exploit his talents; yet she was sure, in the way women are always sure of what can't be proven yet is clear to them alone, that the few moments they had spent together were as welcome to Jones in his aloneness as they were to Lara in hers.

For what seemed to her a long time he stared at the distant blue mountains. Then he said, "The micro sculptures. Would you like to see how they're made?"

Her smile grew slowly, from small to huge. "Oh yeah," she said.

+ + +

What she saw through the magnifying lenses—one for each eye, resembling a pair of blunted binoculars—reminded her of one of those cigar store Indians she had seen pictured in history books, so massive and majestic did it look. It was an exquisite carving: a handsome head held nobly, the proud posture of a chieftain in ceremonial feathered headdress, exquisite detail evident in the chiseled features of the face of red clay, a sculpture not quite complete. Jones lifted an instrument and eased Lara to the side so that he could share one of the viewing lenses with her, and as she watched through the other she saw an amazing apparition: a sculpting blade moved into her view, and it looked impossibly huge in comparison. The flaws in the steel of the scalpel showed like canyons on the moon.

Jones removed the blade from her view and stepped back so that Lara could look through both lenses again. "This is a practice model," he said. "I try to get the residents in here to experiment with the technique, and I start them on oversized pieces."

"Oversized?" Lara wondered, looking through the magnifiers at the noble chieftain. "How large is this?"

"The chief here is about the size of an exclamation point, in standard type." He flipped on the light of a microscope on the lab table. "This one is a bit smaller. It would fit inside a period."

She pulled back from the magnifiers, shot a disbelieving glance at him, and leaned to look through the microscope. What she saw there was a statue of Thomas Jefferson, standing within the rotunda of the Jefferson Memorial. The carving looked so real that she spoke in a whisper, as if not to disturb him. "Jefferson . . ."

"Can you read the inscription?"

She pulled back from the microscope. "You're kidding."

He just looked at her. She peered back into the lenses and dialed the scope around to change the view. And sure enough, the inscription on the sculpted walls around the clay Jefferson came into focus. She read, "*I have sworn upon the altar of God . . .*" She pulled back, startled. "Show-off."

"It's all about touch. Surgeons are taught to see and think, but to work like this you've got to feel. Want to try it?" He picked up a tiny probe and extended it to her. Seeing her hesitate, he smiled and urged, "Come on. You can practice on Chief Red Wing."

Lara's heart was thumping—was it the challenge of the carving or the way he was guiding her hand?—as she pushed a blade, the tiny probe, looking huge in magnification, closer to the half-finished sculpture of the noble Indian. The probe was trembling noticeably, and Lara backed from the lenses, shaking her head. "It's so small . . ."

"Just rest the edge against the base of the statue first," he said in the same voice he had used to calm the young surgeon earlier. He leaned in to a second set of monitoring lenses, also trained on the clay model—and watched her following his instructions. He could tell instantly that she had great skill in her hands. "Good—that's very good! I haven't seen anybody do that on their first try. Okay, now, before you move the edge, listen to your heartbeat."

"My what?"

"Your hearing's good, isn't it?"

She looked at him and said loudly, "HUH?!"

He grinned; she was good at this, good enough to joke while doing it. "We can all hear our hearts beat; we just don't. But for this you have to listen."

She peered through the lenses again, returned the blade to the base of the statue, and used all her will-power to focus on holding the cutting blade perfectly still, against such a tiny object, and listening to her heart. "I can't hear it!"

"Yes, you can. You feel it more than hear it, but you can hear it too, if you focus more on the listening than on the keeping still."

She was trying so hard that sweat was forming on her forehead. For a moment he thought she had given up, like so many of his students did when confronted with a challenge they didn't believe they could master. Then he saw it: she took on a kind of trance, like Jones showed in the operating room; and as she did this, he glanced up from his magnifiers and studied her face.

He spoke in a soothing voice. "Now lift the blade and hold it with just a slight gap between it and the chief's headdress." He looked into the microscope again. "See how the blade moves with each of your heartbeats? Find the rhythm; it'll help you focus."

She cleared her mind of everything except her heart-beat; the blade steadied.

"Good," he whispered. "Now, in the interval between the beats . . . shave off that rough edge of the headdress."

They both watched through the magnifiers as she succeeded. "I did it!" she yelled.

"You sure did."

"This is so great, Andrew! I—" And in an instant, as she forgot the vastness of the microscope's magnification, the blade decapitated the statue. She winced and pulled back from the lenses. "I jerked," she said softly.

"No, you didn't. Your hand was steady. It was your heart. It beat faster and changed your rhythm. Not much. Just enough to cut off Red Wing's head."

Their eyes were locked on each other.

Then Jones's beeper went off.

+ + +

Lara kept pace with him now, at his shoulder as Jones strode quickly into the Emergency Room; they found it strangely quiet, with the ER nurse at her desk. Her name tag said "Carolyn" and her hair was gray, and still she looked as if she could wrestle a three-hundred-pound drunk onto an examination table. "You page me?" Jones asked her.

"A call came in from the mountain." She handed Jones a message slip, and as he read it she added, "I've called one of the orderlies to drive you."

"No, I can do it," he said in that eye-of-the-storm voice already familiar to Lara. He turned to her and said, "I'm sorry to cut the evening short, Dr. Blair—"

The ER nurse told Jones, "By my count you haven't been to bed in forty-eight hours."

"I can do it, Carolyn."

But Nurse Carolyn was tough enough to argue—with patients, with hospital administrators, and especially with a doctor she admired enough to pray for every night, right after the AA meetings she'd been going to for the last seventeen years. "Dr. Jones—"

"I'm fine, Nurse, thank you."

The nurse shoved a packed medical satchel across the desk for him. As Jones took it he patted her on the hand, then moved quickly toward the double doors leading to the parking lot. Lara was still at his side. When he looked at her she said, "Let me drive you."

He paused for a moment; even in his hurry, he paused; and Lara knew he was doing more than just considering her offer. "That won't be necessary," he said with a gentleness that struck Lara as almost . . . sad.

"I'm not going home until we've finished our talk."

Jones paused another moment, taking in her determination.

+ + +

The twenty-year-old station wagon waddled down 29-South from Charlottesville, curling toward the mountains, the headlights soaked up in the heavy darkness of tree-lined turns and rises and dips where the road disappeared. The station wagon was Jones's, but Lara was at the wheel, the rumble of open highway feeling both unaccustomed and welcome to the palms of her hands. When they first left the parking lot Jones watched her carefully to see how she handled the weight and sway of the old suspension, but he saw quickly that Lara was comfortable, even delighted, to be driving, and slowly he began to relax.

He directed her to an exit that sent them right, toward the Blue Ridge, and told her, "Just stay on this road south till you hit Greenstone Mountain Road."

The night was quiet, the heater warm and humming. The edge of anxiety about the agenda that brought her here had begun to melt away, and Lara found herself settling into this moment, strangely free from the past and unconcerned with the future. It was a peace she had not felt since . . . since she did not remember when, and she did not try to remember; she did not want this peace to fade.

Beside her, Jones seemed to feel it too. His body had been taut in the hospital; now he swayed easily with the turns of the road.

And Lara found herself wanting not so much to recruit him as to know him. From that place of ease she asked, "You teach, work double shifts . . . and you still travel?"

"I'm their doctor," he said, his eyes directed toward the range of western mountains, a rolling layer of black beneath the star-flecked sky.

"You haven't been to bed in two days?"

"I don't like to sleep much."

"Just listen to the tires sing. Maybe you can get a nap." As she said this she noticed how soothing her voice had become. She had always liked Jones's voice, resonant like a cello, with Southern softness in his accent; now Lara realized that her own voice had become gentle, even caring. She had not heard those qualities in her voice in a very long time.

Jones rubbed his eyes and stifled a yawn. "You okay?"

"I love to drive." She smiled, looking up through the windshield at the barren tree branches stretching out from the roadside and mingling with the stars. "Once, coming back from college, I took a turn that I knew wasn't the way home and just drove. Blacktop and trees and me at the wheel. Going nowhere, feeling I was going everywhere. Three days. I wanted to keep going. But my father was worried and my mother was . . ." She hesitated; she didn't tell people about her mother. But Jones was different. She glanced to him—

And she saw he had nodded off. For a minute she drove along in a deep silence. Then she found herself smiling.

+ + +

The road wound higher into the mountains. Lara shifted the steering wheel with smooth grace, and the old station wagon floated peacefully. Jones's head, heavy with sleep, rolled with the winding road.

It seemed to Lara that every memory of this road was programming his subconscious—she thought of people as systems to be fixed when they were broken, machines to be refined—and she told herself that his falling asleep was a compliment because it indicated his reliance on her. She knew he did not rely on many people, because the people close to him—Janet in his office, Carolyn in the Emergency Room—were both strong and confident, the kind of people you could trust to get things done. Lara hoped he was coming to trust her, or she would never convince him to come to work for her company.

Still, Lara was a woman, and she found Jones attractive, and his falling asleep when alone with her scraped at the edges of her ego. She liked to pretend that the human mechanical system named Lara Blair was not plagued by feminine vanities and especially not by romantic desires, but as she drove Jones's station wagon into the deepening darkness of the mountains she found feelings rising within her that she could neither accept nor explain.

And there was one more feeling in the stew beginning to bubble inside Lara, in the soul of this woman who did not believe she had a soul. She felt joy. She did not try to find a name for the feeling, and that was part of its wonder: it took root and grew in her because she made no attempt to label or control it. But it was there; she, Lara Blair, principal owner and CEO of Blair Bio-Medical Engineering, had found herself somewhere she had never expected to be: in a decrepit station wagon, driving into hillbilly country, next to a surgeon who would not operate, a doctor with skinned knees and grass stains on his elbows, and she found every moment with him to be intensely exciting and he, on the other hand, had fallen asleep the moment he felt the quiet and the steady rhythm of the road into the mountains. Lara smiled again. Here in Virginia, she was smiling often.

Maybe it was the air. Or the stars. Or the hum of the road. She could understand why Jones slept; it was peaceful here.

+ + +

Jones opened his eyes and tried to rub the sleep from them. He glanced over at Lara just as she was nodding off.

Before he could speak to her or grab at the wheel, he heard the blast of a truck horn and saw the glare of the headlights. Lara woke, screamed, jerked the wheel, but it was too late. A tractor-trailer truck blasting along the other side of the highway had swung too wide on a turn and was surging across the center line into their lane. Impossibly it went airborne. . . . For a moment, the huge truck seemed to pause in the air; then it flew down and slammed into them with a flash.

Inside the station wagon, Jones's scream ripped into the night—

Lara, sitting peacefully at the wheel, jumped, startled by Jones's shout—but she kept the station wagon perfectly steady on the otherwise empty road. He'd been dreaming.

Jones's mind clawed its way out of the nightmare. He gulped air, sweating, his eyes darting as he reconnected with the waking world.

He didn't say anything; what could he say? He settled back again, and she drove on, silent for a long moment, until she said, "No wonder you don't like to sleep."

8

AN HOUR LATER THE MISTS WERE RISING from the forest floor and the station wagon was crossing the bridge over a mountain river, entering a hillbilly hamlet: a post office, a store, a church, all shuttered against the foggy night. There were a few wooden houses, but most of the dwellings were house trailers.

Jones, wide awake since his nightmare, told her, "Just before the church."

Lara turned in at an unpaved driveway through a bare patch of ground next to the white wooden sanctuary, where a handpainted sign nailed into the dirt like a real estate marker said: CLINIC. The clinic was contained in what people of Lara's social circle in Chicago would call "manufactured housing." In Virginia they referred to it as a "double-wide." It was a house trailer.

Lara Blair, in her entire life, had never been to any place like this one. A bare lightbulb burned beneath the tin disk of its rain shield, suspended over the cinder blocks that served as steps in front of the clinic's metal door, once painted white and now a rusty beige in the blare of the bulb. Behind the church was a small cemetery; Lara had seen the gravestones, their stark shadows swinging around them from the headlights of the station wagon as she turned in beside the clinic. The church itself was simple, three arched windows along the side that faced the clinic and—Lara assumed—three more on the opposite side. No stained glass, just clear panes, dark now; but the church must have been busy on Sunday mornings, at least, for the path to its front door was worn bare of grass, and its paint seemed to be the most recent of any other she could see. On up the hill, farther up the road they had just turned off of, stood a store with gas pumps outside, and across the road from that was a shed surrounded by cars in various stages of repair or dismantling, Lara could not tell which. Beyond the store and the shed she could see a couple of houses, and nothing she saw except the church had worn new paint in years.

They parked and stretched; Lara had kept herself trim through treadmills and Pilates and all the exercises an executive can do in isolation; now the stiffness in her limbs reminded her that the chores of everyday people, tasks as simple as driving for hours on end instead of being driven, were more demanding than people in boardrooms and penthouses understood.

Jones led Lara up the cinder-block stairs and through the rusted door, into the makeshift clinic. More bare lightbulbs glared from the metal ceiling. By the entrance a two-hundred-pound woman sat beside a metal table. She wore the kind of hose that are designed to reach the bottom of her knees; she had them rolled to her ankles. "Nell," Jones greeted her easily. "This is Dr. Blair."

"Ma'am." Nell nodded to Lara and appraised her quickly—the mountain people clearly were particular about who stepped into their space, and Lara felt they were particularly particular about any woman near Dr. Jones. To Jones, Nell said, "I wouldn'ta called except—"

"It's okay; what've we got?"

Nell nodded toward two old farmers on a bench near the door; one had a dangling arm. Nell said, "Allen went by Sam's and found him on the porch, limp as a dishrag." Then Nell's eyes—surrounded by pockets of fat but deep green and bright in the glow of the bulbs, shifted toward the shadows at the far end of the room, where a mountain girl no more than seventeen held a crying baby; a second toddler daughter clung to her leg. "And Mona . . . it was Carl again."

Jones moved to the farmers seated against the wall; Lara followed and stopped behind him, close enough to hear, far enough not to intrude. "Mr. Sam?" Jones said.

The farmer did not look up, and his buddy beside him said, "He's scared."

"I ain't," Sam, the farmer, said. Jones gently probed Sam's lifeless hand, and shined a light into his eyes.

"He's 'fraid he's gonna die like Dalton," the buddy, Allen, said.

This prompted Sam to explain, "Dalton fell dead in his lettuce patch. And the dad-gum gophers et off his dad-gum *parts*!"

Nell barked from across the room, "You and Allen hush up that cussin', Sam!"

Lara bit her cheeks to keep from laughing and watched as Sam mouthed in silent emphasis to Jones, ". . . *his dad-gum parts!*" and Allen, who was not cussing but clearly was an accomplice in Nell's mind, nodded gravely in confirmation.

Jones opened his medical bag for his instruments to continue examining Sam, and Lara's gaze fell on the toddler clinging to her mother's skirts at the far end of the room. The toddler had yellow hair and blue eyes that stared like a lost doll's. Lara moved over, sat down in the metal folding chair beside the mother, and ran her fingers through the toddler's hair.

Something happened in Lara's face as she touched the toddler with one hand and squeezed the swaddled baby's foot with the other. Jones glanced at her; their eyes met for a moment. Lara became self-conscious and turned her attention to the young mother, Mona. She was trying to keep her face turned away from everyone, even her children; but feeling the steadiness of Lara's look, Mona lifted her face enough for Lara to see the bloody contusion on her cheek. It was the kind of bruise a fist makes.

Lara winced, involuntarily. Then she reached out. Mona recoiled, more ashamed than hurt. But Lara persisted, and Mona allowed her to probe the damage to her cheek. Lara stepped to Jones's medical bag and found what she needed to clean and bandage the wound.

Jones had come to a conclusion with Sam; he knelt

to be eye to eye with the old mountaineer. "Mr. Sam, you've had a stroke," he said.

"Will it kill me?" Sam asked, unflinching.

Just as plainly Jones answered, "Hasn't yet. I need you to come to Charlottesville."

"I ain't goin' to no hospital."

"I'll be there with you," Jones said. "Hey, it's either me or the gophers."

"Allen'll drive me," Sam answered, and in those few words Lara heard exactly how deeply these people trusted Jones.

"Nell," he said, "call the hospital and tell 'em to admit Mr. Sam here for a full cranial scan."

As Nell was picking up the phone, the door banged open and a lean redneck stained with beer and motor oil clomped into the room. He snapped at Mona, and presumably at the children too, though to Lara it seemed he didn't notice them at all, "Ya'll come on." To Lara he barked, "Leave her alone, she ain't hurt! Come on!" He pulled at Mona, who shied back from him.

When he reached again, Lara stood. "Get away from her," she said, quietly and clearly.

The confrontation, the look in Carl's eyes, or maybe the look in Lara's, frightened Mona. Carl saw her fear, and it confirmed his sense of power. What Carl did not worry about was Jones, who seemed to be ignoring him, simply drawing a syringe and vial from his bag. Carl barked out to the whole place, as if to defy the contempt in their faces, "She let the kids run in the yard! They pulled the tarp off my tools, and it rained on my power saw! Made it short out!"

"So you hit her," Lara said quietly, her eyes more still than they ever were in the boardroom.

Carl, staring at Lara as if to dare her to challenge him, advanced toward Mona, talking to her through his clenched teeth even as he kept his eyes on Lara. "Come on, I done told you! Come— Ow!" He reacted to the jab of the hypodermic into the muscle where his neck met his back and jerked around to see Jones holding the dripping syringe like a dagger. Before the surprise of the injection had left his mind, a reaction began to flood through his body. "What . . . what . . . ?" Carl muttered. Sweat suddenly beaded on Carl's face; it began pouring from him. And he backed to the door, spun to get his head outside, and began retching.

Jones moved up behind him and said matter-of-factly, "It's a virus I took from a cadaver at the University morgue."

Carl retched harder, painfully.

"A cadaver—you know, a dead body. It was full of pus, died from a virus. Right now that virus is working its way into your bones, and no other doctor in this whole world knows the cure except me."

"You're lying!" Carl sputtered, more pleading than insisting. He straightened himself against the pain, gripping his chest where his heart hammered against his ribs; sweat poured from his face and soaked his shirt, and Carl felt hotter than he would have with malarial fever.

Jones still spoke casually. "Six months from now, if she tells me you've been good, I'll give you the antidote. You hurt her again and I'll let your whole brain turn to pus." Carl lurched out the door and flopped down the steps like a trout on a creek bank, then staggered on rubbery legs halfway to his pickup truck, where he fell again.

Everyone in the clinic was stone quiet.

Nell broke the silence, lifting a brown paper sack toward Jones. "These cakes are for you," she said.

9

JONES INSISTED ON DRIVING BACK, and on the winding road down the mountain Lara spoke for the first time since they left the clinic. "Adrenaline, right?" she said.

Jones nodded.

"I've never seen nausea like that."

"With a gut full of liquor, a jolt of adrenaline nearly always makes you puke. I've had some experience with drunken fistfights."

"I'll watch your whole brain turn to pus?" She was laughing, shaking her head.

He grinned. "That was a good touch, huh? You hungry? Open that sack."

She opened the sack and pulled out chocolate brownies. "They pay you in brownies?"

"That land the church and clinic are on was once part of a little farm my great-grandparents owned. My grandmother gave the land to build the church. My parents died when I was in high school. When I went off to college those old farmers like Sam worked the land so I could go to school without selling the only thing my folks could leave me."

Lara stared out the passenger side window. The moon was rising, half full and stark white, and it followed them through the passing tree tops. "So how many brownies do I need to give you to come to work for us?" she said. For a long moment she did not speak, just felt his stillness beside her; then she turned to him. "You come to work for my company and I'll fund that clinic. Give them a doctor."

"They've got a doctor."

"Two doctors—full time. Permanent buildings. Nurses. Just tell me what you want, and you've got it."

Jones stared at the dark road, as if he hadn't heard. Then, as if it was an answer, he said, "It's right up here."

+ + +

Jones pulled off the pavement at a spot where the road curved, almost doubling back on itself. He stopped the station wagon and got out. Lara, intrigued, followed him as he walked along the road shoulder until he paused and stared out where the asphalt caught the silvery cast of the moon.

"Her name was Faith," he said. "We met in Med School. The last summer of our surgical residencies we did Europe on eighty-five dollars a day, and I proposed to her there. We were going to get married in the fall."

Jones knew there was so much of the story he was leaving out; an endless well of details and stories about Faith flooded through his soul and surged now, wanting him to spill them out: the way he had first noticed her hair, reddish brown like the mane of a chestnut horse, shining two rows in front of him as he sat in the lecture hall of their first class together; the way dimples flanked her mouth and caused him always to feel her face was just about to break into a smile; the way her eyes were always so still when anyone else was talking—a distinguished medical school lecturer, a friend, a waitress, a truck driver, a sick patient, or that patient's worried family member—Faith listened to all of them with the same care and the same intensity. But Jones tried now to focus on the barest bones of the story because he couldn't tell the story of what had happened at this spot without seeing it all again with his memory, as vividly as he saw it with his eyes: the car rolling along the highway, Faith driving, Jones finishing his call on the cell phone. That's why he didn't talk about it, why he hadn't brought anyone with him to this place or explained it like he was doing now. But Lara Blair had something about her, a kind of ruthlessness when it came to facts. She had the guts to tell him what she wanted and how determined she was to get it. Jones couldn't give her what she wanted; he had been conscious of that from the beginning. And after this night he expected never to see her again. All of this, he understood. Still he admired her, and he wanted to tell someone—to tell *her*. And why that was, he did not understand.

He forced himself forward with his story. "The clinic was Faith's idea. We were on this road, driving up for the weekend."

Lara listened, seeing the whole thing through Jones's eyes.

"You know how people in an accident often have no memory of it?" he asked and waited for Lara to nod; he needed to know she was grasping it all as he went, for he wasn't sure he could keep going if he lost momentum and had to sink into the event rather than simply describe its surface. "Well, sometimes I wish that's how it could be for me. I remember everything, even the moments leading up to it. I was feeling like I owned the world—the young surgeon with a touch like no one else's . . ." And then Jones actually shuddered as he remembered Faith smiling at him that night, when he took her hand. "And . . ." he went on, "with a love like no one else's."

At that moment in Jones's exquisitely detailed memory, an airborne tractor trailer truck flew out of nowhere and smashed into Faith's side of the car. He saw the windshield breaking, her hands gripping the wheel; he even saw in his memory what he could not imagine he had seen with his eyes, yet it was all so vivid: those dimples freezing at the edges of that mouth that loved to smile so much and would never smile again. He saw the world start tumbling, in a tumult of grinding, screaming metal.

He looked hard at Lara now, to see her face instead of the memories. "They told me later that they thought the truck driver had swerved to avoid a deer and had lost control, then jumped the center divider. From just over there." He pointed to the spot. He stood there taking deep slow breaths, and Lara knew he could still see it all.

And he did see it: all the chaos after the wreck. His body on the side of the road. The trailer truck crumpled in the trees beyond him. A few cars that had stopped, their panicky owners darting about and shouting, a siren wailing in the distance.

"I found myself on the pavement, with people yelling, 'Get a doctor!'" He paused again. "Get a doctor. I think that's what brought me around. Get a doctor." He paused once more. "Faith was still in the car."

Now the memories were at their most hellish. He saw the mangled mass that had been their jeep, and the headlights of the other cars shooting helter-skelter through the darkness around the wreckage as he wobbled to his feet, the Good Samaritans who had stopped to help trying to keep him down; but in his memory he pushed them away and struggled through the knot of people at the wreckage of the car. As the onlookers saw him, staggering and bloody, they tried to hold him back. And Jones commanded their compliance with the magic words that had worked for centuries: "I'm a doctor!" They parted, and he looked down in horror.

Lara listened, absolutely still, watching him as he stood there paler than the moonlight, the images flashing through his mind in a nightmare he could not wake from. His face grew whiter as the voice inside him—his own voice—rose louder: "Faith! Faith!" And Faith, lying sideways inside the upside-down car, did not respond, and he tried to compose himself and deal with the crisis.

Somehow the memory of this struggle enabled him to go on with telling the story aloud. "The first thing I became aware of, on a medical basis, was the volume of blood she had lost. She was cold from the shock, her larynx was crushed, and she couldn't breathe." He saw himself grab at one of the onlookers and yell, *"A knife! I need a knife!"* One of the onlookers produced a large pocket knife. Jones snapped it open, and turned back to Faith, limp and bloody in the mangled car.

"She had to have a tracheotomy," Jones told Lara.

At that moment they were interrupted as a pickup came rolling up the mountain, its headlights making them blink. Seeing them stopped at the side of the road, the driver slowed and rolled down his window. "You folks all right?" he called out.

"Just fine," Jones called back. "Just taking a break. Thanks for checking." The driver waved and pulled away again, and Lara welcomed the return of the quiet and the darkness.

"I tried to put everything out of my head except

what I had to do," Jones said, his voice steady enough, though Lara thought she felt—felt more than heard—it tremble. "I pushed in the knife . . . and just as I cut into her windpipe . . ."

In his memory Jones saw Faith's eyes spring open. And her eyes were fixed directly on him.

He stared at Lara—or stared toward her, for what he saw was Faith's eyes, looking so deeply into his own.

His voice lowered; it was barely higher than the sound of the wind drifting through the trees. He asked Lara, "Have you ever seen someone die?"

Lara nodded. "My mother," she said. "And father."

Jones nodded; that knowledge of Lara's, that awareness of what it was like to lose someone you love absolutely, was surely part of the reason he could tell her all he was telling her now. "It wasn't what I saw that haunts me. It's what I felt. Through the handle of that knife, I felt the life leave her body."

Jones stopped talking then. His eyes were wet circles, but tears were not what blinded him; for the next two minutes all he saw was that other night at this same spot on this road, when he dropped the knife, knowing it and all his skill were useless now. In his memory he hugged Faith's limp form as her blood dripped upon the postcard of Creation, lying on the upended ceiling of the shattered car.

Lara was barely breathing herself. Jones seemed unaware that she was there; until that moment she had felt that he was talking directly and uniquely to her. When he spoke again it was as if he was talking only to himself. "I feel it still," he muttered.

He looked once more at Lara. His face was changing; she could see the memory gathering itself again, back into that dark place where he tried to keep it hidden. He went on, the words flowing. "So that's why I can't help you, Dr. Blair. I can set a broken arm or sew a cut. I can still carve little statues. But I can't use a surgical instrument on living flesh, because when I do I feel Faith dying."

There wasn't any more for Lara to hear. And she had no words to speak, until they were driving down the mountain once again.

10

JONES, IT SEEMED TO LARA as she sat in the passenger seat beside him and he drove easily down the mountain, almost casually now, seemed more at peace than before. But Lara was haunted, even more than when they left the roadside ten minutes before. A shock had hit her and had grown rather than fading like the sting of any other blow might, and it wasn't just the collapse of her agenda that she felt. She knew she had just come face to face with a force beyond her understanding, and it belonged to a realm beyond the questions of science that she did not yet know how to answer but would solve someday. This was a mystery that Lara knew she would never answer. Yet still she asked. "After that . . . how did you go on?"

"I suppose some people could say I haven't gone on. I put one foot in front of another, but most of the time it seems to me I've gone backwards. For a while," he said, "I drank." He stared at the road ahead, where the headlights bore into the darkness. It was an hour past midnight, and they seemed the only travelers on the face of the whole earth. When he spoke again, Lara wasn't sure if was talking to her or just talking, just telling the truth. "Faith . . . had this belief—it seemed so original to her, but she always said it came from the Bible, though millions of people have read it and not come to the same conclusion she did. It was a method she saw, that something in her spirit saw, and she said it was a way to clean your soul and make life worth living. So I try it. Especially when times are the blackest. And it's kept me going."

"Can you tell me what it is?"

"It's easy to talk about, but it's much harder to do, but you can't think yourself through it, you just have to do it to know whether it works. She believed that the best way to do a good deed was to do it in secret. If you commit an act of charity and people know you did it, it drains away the true power of the deed. If someone unknown does evil to you, you start suspecting everyone around you of harboring hate, and you hate back. But if you're on the receiving end of a truly anonymous act of love, you begin to suspect people around you, maybe even strangers, maybe the whole world, of caring for you. You learn to believe."

"Faith was the perfect name for her."

Jones looked at Lara, surprised by that haunting phrase. "Yes," Jones said. "Yes, it was."

Lara thought about all the checks she had written to charities, and the praise they had given her, and the strange brew of annoyance, guilt, and obligation she felt each time they contacted her with more appeals. She thought about the way fund-raisers played to the egos of their donors: the silver circle of givers, the gold circle, the platinum circle, the Chairman's Group. Lara's name and that of her company appeared often on the honor rolls of many charities, all of them respectable groups (and all of them chosen carefully by Blair Bio-Med's public relations director to enhance the company's reputation as well as its political associations). But none of that kind of giving had ever infused Lara with a sense of personal connection to any kind of internal force. She found herself wanting to argue with the concept. "What about leadership?" she asked. "We need charities, many of them—probably most of them—do good work, and sometimes somebody's got to step forward publicly and stir other people up to do the right thing by showing them how."

"Well, sure. Sometimes people are going to know who's done something that they're glad got done. It was Faith's idea to build the clinic in the mountains, not mine. Everybody thought it was me because it was in my home town, next to the church my grandmother founded, on the ground my granddaddy gave. But it wasn't my idea to put the trailer up there and drive there every weekend and see the people who were too afraid to go to doctors in the city, or too ashamed, or just plain too ignorant and poor. The clinic's a good thing and it's a public thing and I love it, and working there gives me the idea that I might be doing some good and the idea's important. But when every hope you have is shattered and you don't know where to find any, and you don't want to live anymore because you can't find love anywhere, that's when you need more than an idea. That's when you need to do something that no one else knows about, or will ever know. Something that you hope will matter, but you can't even be sure of that. It's got to be something that costs you—not just money or time, it costs you your own expectation of a reward. But you do that, you give up your pride, you give up your own secret demand that you are God and you make the rules of life, then you do get a reward: the experience that life is worth something, that it's a gift, that someone else gave to you."

Jones took a deep breath. He let it out. He looked at Lara, and then he looked back at the road again. "She was right. There's a price to faith. I've learned to pay it."

+ + +

The pink light of dawn fell faintly on the white wings of the Blair Bio-Med jet as Jones pulled up close to it, outside the private hangars beside the Charlottesville Airport runway. He stopped, stepped out quickly, and opened the door.

All that we've gone through in the last twenty-four hours, Lara thought, *and he's still such a gentleman.*

Jones retrieved her bag from the truck and together they moved up to the step at the jet's door; she turned to him, and not knowing anything better to do, she shook his hand. "Well. Thanks for . . . taking the time to talk with me," she said.

"No. Thank you." For a moment their eyes met, and his were steadier, stronger, more direct than they had been the first time they had looked at each other. She stepped up into the plane, turned to face him again, then backed away from the plane's door as the flight attendant started to swivel it closed; but Jones interrupted, moving into the doorway. "Dr. Blair—that Lincoln carving. I gave it to the museum two days ago. You had time to look up my resume. But you couldn't know about my taste for Russian literature, not in time to read up on it."

Not only Lara but also the flight attendant and the copilot of the jet were wondering what he was getting at.

Jones, Lara was learning, never stopped thinking, and when he spoke it was because he was sure of something. His eyes boring into her, he said, "You act as if everything is a cold, calculated decision for you. But you've read Russian literature on your own. You must've, your name's Lara—you're named after a character in *Doctor Zhivago*! You're poetic and warm and . . . when you touch a baby something beautiful happens in your eyes. But you pretend as if life is business. Why is that?"

She was still looking at him as the jet door closed.

+ + +

The copilot of the Blair Bio-Med jet was a lanky young man who began his career as a mechanic in the Air

National Guard, but the pilot was a woman named—delightfully, to Lara—Angelica. Angelica was forty and became a pilot by using the Blair Employee Education Program to pay for part of her flight training and work her way up from receptionist in the headquarters lobby. Lara herself had approved the unusual education request, saying that any woman named Angelica was destined to learn to fly, and since Angelica's training began she had shown a special fondness for her boss. Whenever Lara took the company jet, Angelica kept the door into the cockpit open, and as the plane bored through the blue atmosphere and the feathery canyons of clouds between the sky and Virginia, she was glancing back at Lara in the mirror above the controls.

Lara caught the glance. She snapped, "What?" But she knew what.

"Nothing, Dr. Blair." Angelica tried to look grim and hide her smirk.

Lara turned her face back toward the window, and sitting there above the clouds, released from work and the world, she let her mind drift . . .

And she dreamed. She was not asleep; she felt more wide awake than ever before. And floating through her mind was a vision. Her body, wrapped in wedding-gown lace, sailing slowly through a world of clouds; weightless, a buoyant ballet from the hidden recesses of Lara's heart . . .

At the beginning of her fantasy, she soared alone, amazed to find herself in her own heaven . . .

But this being her heaven, she was not alone. As her body turned, there was now a baby snuggled against her chest—a baby with blue eyes like the girl at the clinic . . .

And drifting through this cloudy nirvana with them was Andrew Jones. He held Lara's outstretched hand, delicately, by the fingertips, swirling through the milky sunlight above the world. It was a scene like Michelangelo might paint.

Lara, Jones, and the baby—their baby, for they are the mother and father—nestled in this bed of a dream sky . . .

Lara stared out the window. She could see it now, those forms dancing across the irises of her eyes.

She closed her eyes, pressing out the images, turning herself away. She had work to do, and she couldn't do it drifting among the clouds.

+ + +

Jones drove through the Virginia countryside in his old station wagon. He headed north of Charlottesville, out into the rolling hill country where people wealthy enough to buy indulgence properties had invested in horse farms; in recent years many Hollywood figures had found themselves drawn to the area and some even lived there full time. Like most things in Virginia, the history of the place worked its way into the bones of even the newly rich, and their homes of stone and timber blended well with the brick colonial houses that echoed Williamsburg and Monticello. The sun was over the horizon now, and bright, but it was still early and there were no cars on the road lined with oaks and hickories, leafless in November.

Most of the older churches in Virginia's wealthiest areas were Episcopal, a reflection of the time two hundred fifty years before, when it was illegal under the rules of the British government for anyone in the Commonwealth to be a member of any other denomination. But not far along the road Jones came to a Lutheran church, built by the descendants of the German immigrants who had brought their skills in mining, glassmaking, woodwork, and horsemanship into the fertile markets of the New World. The church was small yet stately, faced entirely with gray stone, beneath a tall slate roof. Jones had always found it quite beautiful.

He stopped on the paved roundabout that served as the church's parking lot, stopped his car, and got out. There was no one around this early in the morning, and no one passed on the road except a pickup truck full of hay bound in tight bales.

Jones walked toward the church, but instead of going in, he moved past the front door and kept walking to the short forest of stone monuments that made up the small cemetery that characterized every old church in Virginia. Without stopping, for he well knew the way, he approached a grave.

Faith's grave.

How her body had come to rest here, in the graveyard of a church she had never attended, was for Jones a curious story of pride mixed with baffling religious prejudice. Faith's father's family had attended a Lutheran church in Pennsylvania, and he had married her mother there; Faith's mother was not religious but—she later told her daughter—she had found the church to be a lovely setting for sprays of flowers and men in tuxedoes and a bride in a white wedding gown. (Jones had learned about all of this directly from Faith when they were dreaming of their own wedding.) Faith's mother had surprised everyone by wanting a traditional wedding—surprised them because she was given to talking about her life-changing experiences at Woodstock, and she wore beads and flowers in her hair long after Faith's father had earned his law degree and started wearing suits to work every day. But the mother was an artist; she formed uniquely shaped pottery and painted unusual picture frames, and Faith's father didn't mind her quirks.

He did mind, however, when his wife grew bored and tired of her life as a lawyer's wife and moved to California, the same month their daughter left home for college. Apparently there was another artist involved, a man Faith's mother talked about when she would phone her at the dormitory. That relationship did not last, for Faith and Andrew, when they traveled out to California to meet Faith's mother when they had returned from their Europe trip and had begun to plan their own wedding, did not meet the man and never heard him mentioned. But the mother remained in California.

Faith's father had died shortly after her graduation from college. When Faith told Andrew about this it was the only time he had ever seen her weep. She said she knew it was illogical but she had always believed that since her father's fondest dream was to see her safely set off into life—to see her "raise her sails," he had told her—he had stayed alive despite the medical condition he had developed when he and Faith's mother had journeyed to India one summer when their daughter was away at a scholastic camp for academically gifted junior high schoolers. While Faith's mother had studied art, yoga, and transcendental meditation, he had worked on a Habitat for Humanity build site; somewhere along the way he contracted hepatitis; later they found liver cancer; a month after he saw his daughter lift her sails and toss her graduation cap into the June sky, he was dead.

They buried him in the graveyard of the Lutheran church he had attended as a boy in Pennsylvania. Faith's mother did not attend the funeral; but, she told Faith, she had performed a ceremony in celebration of her father's life with some friends in California who had never met her father but who were acquainted with his higher energies.

Jones kept these facts to himself; on their surface they would, he knew, make Faith's mother sound shallow and soulless to most of the people he knew. Sometimes, of course, she seemed exactly that way to him. She was the mother of the woman Jones loved; but it was not just respect for Faith that caused Jones to keep the facts about her mother private. Jones knew the woman did have a heart; he heard it break, on the terrible day when he had to make the phone call to California to tell her about the accident that had taken her daughter's life.

Faith's mother flew back from California, her first return to the East Coast since she had left her husband seven years before. When she saw Andrew she collapsed into his arms and wept, and it didn't matter then that Andrew had grown up hearing his grandmother sing "The Old Rugged Cross" and his almost-mother-in-law had spent the last decade chanting in an ashram; they grieved for the love of the same beautiful life, and the truth was that they leaned on each other.

It was when time came for them to choose Faith's final resting place that problems arose. Her mother favored cremation and the spreading of the ashes in some sacred grove—though she was not able to articulate just where that grove might be, or what would have made it sacred to Faith. Jones's preference was to have Faith laid to rest in the cemetery beside the church in the mountains, next to the clinic Faith had founded; it was where Jones intended to be buried someday. But his desires, no matter how deep and heartfelt, had no legal standing; he and Faith had not yet married, and her mother was the closest blood relative. She never fully insisted on a New

Age sort of ceremony and a cremation after, but it was clear to Jones that the idea of Faith being interred in the ground of a church in Appalachia threatened every one of her mother's cultural assumptions. Her mother never used the word God, even to apply it as if it meant simply *a* god. She spoke of Spirit, and did not seem to feel that Spirit existed in the shadow of the evergreens up in hillbilly country.

They were at an impasse until one lonely night outside the funeral home, when Jones took her to dinner and Faith's mother confided to him that none of her friends from California were going to come out to join her for the ceremony. They sent their Highest Intentions and Celebrations, but they couldn't come. But some friends and relatives from Pennsylvania were coming. And Jones saw then in her face the agonies that she felt. Those people would not care for a mythical grove or a sacred circle and wishes to Spirit; they wanted something more familiar, more comforting to them; and yet Jones knew that this was a moment when Faith's mother could not be disregarded, no matter what he felt himself, because what he felt most was that Faith owned all his love, and she had loved her mother, so her mother's wishes mattered.

Then he remembered that Faith's mother and father

had married in a Lutheran church. At dinner he did an Internet search on his cell phone and found the stone church in the horse country. He suggested they ask the parishioners if they might find a spot in their hearts and their cemetery for girl who had lost her life while driving into the mountains to give medical care to strangers; something told Jones they were sure to say yes.

"But Andrew," Faith's mother had muttered, her voice shaking as she sat at the formica table of a Waffle House and wrapped her trembling fingers around her coffee cup, "I never took her to a Lutheran church. I never took her to any church at all."

Jones reached out and took her fingers from the coffee cup and held them in his hands and looked into her frightened, anguished eyes. "But somehow," he said quietly, "she came to believe in what they taught there. And every night, she prayed for you."

Now Jones sat down on the stone bench at the foot of her plot. The air was sharply colder than the day before, and he didn't seem to notice.

+ + +

When Lara had sent the text message telling her inner circle that she would be staying overnight, a sense of excitement had spread from them through the Blair Bio-Med command team; something was happening, they could all feel it. Brenda called Malcolm at home to ask if Lara had called him or sent any further word; Malcolm told her he had heard nothing else and he was sure if Lara wanted to confide anything of a feminine nature then she would do it to Brenda, not to him. Brenda insisted she had been thinking only of business; didn't Malcolm interpret her delay as promising? They speculated for a while, with Brenda musing about how much good a relationship would do for Lara and how Dr. Jones seemed on paper to be exactly the kind of man whom she could both respect and admire, the kind of man who would intrigue her. Malcolm countered that whoever people seemed to be on paper usually had little to do with how they were in person, and besides all that, the crucial issue was whether or not he could perform the surgical techniques they were searching for so desperately. Brenda answered that Lara could tell in a heartbeat the difference between Dr. Jones's resume and his personal presence and something was promising about him; why else would Lara have stayed?! On and on they went, knowing nothing, wondering everything.

There was no further word until they checked their

cell phones first thing the next morning and found text messages telling them their boss was flying back. Both of them drove straight to work. As soon as Brenda learned that Lara had arrived in the building she hurried down the corridor to her office.

As she reached the door Malcolm, just coming out, passed her, muttering.

Brenda entered the reception area of Lara's office and walked by Juliet, Lara's secretary; they exchanged conspiratorial glances, and Juliet shook her head. Brenda moved on into Lara's main office and found her at her desk, trying to lose herself in brain scans and schematics for machine designs. Brenda bounced in and plopped down in a chair. "Soooo? How'd it go?"

Lara did not look up. "He can't do it."

"Can't? Or won't?"

"Won't, can't, what's the difference?" Lara said flatly, still sorting through her paperwork.

"So what's he like?"

Lara shot her an impatient look. "I wasn't there to find out what he was like. I was there to recruit him for our surgical development program."

"You were there a long time." Brenda waited, but got no response. "You look tired. Was the hotel bad?

Because I tried to call you several times through the night, and they said you weren't there."

"We were in a car."

"In a car."

"On a drive. Out in the country . . ."

"Out in the country! Sounds like a wonderful time! Sounds romantic. Sounds like a date!"

"No, it—he can't do it, Brenda. He can't. Now if you'll excuse me, we have experiments to set up." Lara strode out of the room.

THE
GIFT

11

TWO WEEKS AFTER Lara Blair came to Virginia and drove up into the mountains to visit the Blue Ridge clinic with Jones, old Sam finally came down from the mountains and showed up at the Charlottesville hospital.

Sam had lived for the last fifty years in an Appalachian valley—the locals called it a holler—so isolated that he had no electricity and no running water; in all that time he had not journeyed to what he call the flatlands. Jones welcomed him and arranged for him to be admitted, though the paperwork was an issue since Sam had never filed for anything from the government and their only records of his life were a driver's license and the records he had filled out when he joined the Army in World

War II. Jones found a place for Allen to stay—Allen said he would be content with the couch in Jones's office, since he planned to spend every moment making sure his oldest and only friend was not poisoned or poked to death by a nurse—and the hospital staff immediately began running tests on Sam.

It was the MRI that scared Sam the most; to be strapped to a moving slab and slid into a coffinlike space that rattled and screamed like the mouth of hell did not comfort Sam; when Jones dropped in to see him just before the procedure, Sam told him, "I don't want to see the Immer Eye."

Jones realized Sam thought the doctors had been talking about something monstrous and tried to reassure him, saying, "Sam, I know the Immer Eye . . . the MRI . . . it sounds bad but there's not a thing this machine can do that will hurt you."

"The feller that wheeled me down here from the room told me to leave my watch cause the Immer Eye would jerk it right outer my pocket and even if it didn't my watch wouldn't never work again if it even got in the same room with the Immer Eye."

"It won't hurt you, Sam. I promise." When Jones saw Sam's eyes, watery and blue like a mountain sky on a foggy morning, look up into his, Jones patted the old man's boney shoulder and said, "Trust me, Sam. I won't let anyone hurt you."

Jones stood and watched as they wheeled Sam into the scanning room. As the door closed Jones was left alone, and his thoughts drifted. To Lara.

+ + +

At the moment that Sam was being slid into the Immer Eye and was yelling out to Allen, waiting for him in the control room, that to him it looked more an Immer Anus, Lara was working at her lab.

Since returning from Virginia she had been even more driven than before—and less patient. No one, least of all Lara herself, doubted that the discovery of the microscopic figurines had given them all reasons to hope that the techniques they had spent so much time and money and effort trying to develop might be more than theoretically possible, but were actually within their grasp. The frustration of that hope had left Lara angry and sensitive to the shortcomings of her staff. The researchers around her—most of them with medical or engineering degrees, or both—had begun to strike her as absorbed, uncaring, even selfish. It did not help her mood when she realized that it was she herself whom she most suspected of such failings.

This afternoon, finding herself unable to concentrate, she shooed everyone away from her; then, left alone, she looked down at a medical journal on her desk. The picture on the cover was of a baby. Lara stared at its eyes, then walked to the window and looked out the window at the clouds, high above her.

+ + +

Jones stood beside the printers in the scanner's photo annex and studied Sam's scans. He waved the radiologist over and pointed to a place on the scan. As the radiologist left him, Jones stared at the scans, and the areas of light and dark on the film were like clouds.

+ + +

Lara worked late at her lab, long after she had told everyone else to quit and go home. She had spent the last several days studying replays of all her failed attempts with the replica brain, and as if that weren't depressing enough she gathered all the Roscoe brains and began taking them apart in order to try to see the problem from the inside out. At least that's what she told everybody; the truth was, she did not know what else to do. It was past midnight when she finally shoved back from her desk, pressed her palms into the sockets of her eyes, stood and moved to the door, shut out the lights, and stepped into the hallway.

She was too tired to take the stairs. She rode the elevator to the top floor, then moved down an empty corridor to the door past her office, where her office apartment lay tucked away. She walked inside, passed directly through the sitting room without turning on the lights, walked into the bedroom, and lay down on the bed. All alone, she stared at the ceiling.

In Lara's lifetime she had studied many topics: biology, mathematics, chemistry, engineering; but she had read poetry too, had learned about art, and some history. She had done a good deal of thinking about ideas and the internal processes of invention, but her investigations of how to open the mind to new thoughts left her feeling as blank and empty as she had felt in disassembling the replica brains in her laboratory. She did not deny the existence of ideas, even now, when she had no new ones; but even when she had fresh inspirations she had never been able to tell where they had come from.

She did feel sure—and thought this plainly as she

lay on the bed of her office apartment and gazed at the acoustic tiles on the ceiling—that one crucial ingredient in having an idea was the belief that some better way of thinking, some truer way of seeing the world, existed. It seemed to Lara that no one could even recognize a good idea if they already believed that no improvement, no positive change, no breakthrough innovation was even possible. She realized for the thousandth time since she had visited Virginia how much her encounter with Jones and his different approach to living had affected her. She could almost see his face in the ceiling above her bed, could almost hear him say, *Believe* is a stronger word than *know*.

Lara asked herself what she believed. And the answer seemed to be: *nothing*.

For years she had hoped—hoped without truly believing—that she would solve the great riddle of brain surgery that had stumped the great researchers who had come before her, that had even stumped her father. She did not examine her hope because it was impossible to keep going without it.

But now, here in the darkness, she asked herself how she could live, hoping for nothing and believing in nothing.

And then she began to think about what Jones had told her that Faith believed.

+ + +

Jones walked alone through the park where he played rugby. He looked up; the stars were shining overhead . . . and the moon was full above the mountains. He stared up at it.

He took a scrap of paper from his pocket and began to write something down.

12

AFTER HIS SHIFT IN THE EMERGENCY ROOM—it was a
quiet night and he got to nap on his cot there—Jones
began the morning in his makeshift carving room,
supervising three young surgical residents as they
worked on their microscopic technique. He sensed
trouble when Stafford entered and moved up to him
quietly. "Dr. Jones . . . ?" Stafford began, then hesitated.

"Hi, Stafford. What's up?"

"I've got a patient, eighty-three years old, on life
support. Her brain activity stopped this morning."

Jones put down his carving tools. He looked at
Stafford, liking him for caring enough to ponder such
a question, to come and ask it. Jones moved him away

from the residents, toward the counter where they left all the carved miniatures to dry, and said, "Somebody's got to tell her family to turn off the machines. And the hospital wants you to do it."

"Yeah."

"And you want me to do it."

"No. Yeah. No. I just . . . need some advice."

"You take the weight off the family. Tell them there's no hope if she stays on the machines, but if you turn them off there's the tiniest chance that her body will come back on its own. Then you give the patient enough morphine that you're sure, for the rest of your life, that she could feel no pain. And you turn off the machines. . . . Do you want me to do it?"

"No. I'll do it." Stafford started to walk away.

"Stafford." Stafford stopped, and looked back to Jones. "Whenever you think back on it, remember the peace you gave them. And the price you paid to do it."

Stafford nodded and walked away. Jones watched him go, and the weight of the moment, of what he had just felt and said, caused him to pause.

He sat down at one of the empty carving stations. He switched on the microscope light and picked up the carving instruments.

+ + +

Lara walked out of the Blair Bio-Med Building, onto a Chicago sidewalk, the medical complex behind her and office buildings in the other three directions. She found herself squinting against the sunlight; it had been a while since she had been outside.

She walked alone down the street. She seemed to remember that there was a church somewhere in the neighborhood, a relic built more than a hundred years ago and spared for its architecture. Halfway down the block she found it—a small cathedral, now stained through years of neglect. She stood on the sidewalk and stared at it for a long moment. An ornamental iron fence surrounded it, but the gate was wide open, and Lara walked inside.

Lara was unfamiliar with the surroundings within the sanctuary; she looked around like any stranger might, taking it all in. The sanctuary was empty except for a few older women saying prayers and a couple of winos sleeping in the pews.

Not far from the rear doors was a box, marked "For the Poor."

Lara moved up beside it. She glanced around to be

sure no one was watching, then withdrew a large envelope from her purse and slipped it into the poor box.

Then she walked out, into the spring sunshine.

Lara walked back toward the Blair Bio-Med Building. There was something different about her—or was it that something was different about the world around her? She noticed the bustle, the people, the energy everywhere; she closed her eyes and felt the sun on her face.

As she reached the building, she noticed that in the planter boxes beside the entrance, the trees were budding, and there, on one, she saw the first blossom of spring.

She stopped to admire that first blossom, to appreciate it, like a prayer.

+ + +

Just before sunset an old priest stubbed out a cigarette in the ashtray beside the holy water and entered the sanctuary. Mechanically he tossed a new carton of candles onto the votive boxes and emptied its coin box, like any other broken-down vender making his rounds.

Working his way to the rear of the church, impatiently waving a drunk out of his way, he reached the poor box and unlocked it. He found the envelope, opened it . . . and stopped short. The envelope was full of thousand-dollar bills.

13

WHEN LARA ARRIVED at her headquarters building the next morning, she felt—felt before she thought it—that something was different around her. Everyone, from the wiry Salvadoran attendant who handled the jumble of cars in their underground parking structure, to Amos, the security guard who stood by the entrance into the main foyer, to the just-out-of-college interns who rode the elevator up with her—all of them seemed changed. Then it struck Lara that the change was in her. Ever since the night before, when she had left the envelope in the poor box, she had felt a surging thrill, had felt it from the moment the envelope had slid from her hand into the dark slit and thudded onto the wood of the bare bottom of the box. She had no name for this feeling; she had never known its sensations, or its perspectives. Last night the world was vivid, and she saw it with clarity. She had thought this to be a temporary elation, brought on by the adrenaline of a new adventure and the sense of the unknown that came with the gift.

Then she had slept with more peace than she had known in years. And now here she was this morning, feeling the same way; and the people around her *did* look happier, brighter, more optimistic, as if somehow, beyond some vast horizon, hope waited for them—all of them, for through some dynamic that Lara did not begin to understand, her gift, unknown to everyone in the world but her, had united her with everybody, even strangers. Hope. Lara had not known real hope for a long, long time. She did not know Hope's true absence, until she felt its coming.

+ + +

It was not just that Lara noticed something different about everyone else; everyone else noticed a change in her. The people at Blair Bio-Medical were like any other herd of humans; they drew their mood from their leader, and most of the time that process was subtle and unconscious, but this morning the transformation in Lara from the heaviness that had smothered her spirit in the last weeks to the lightness that lifted her along as she moved down the corridors was unmistakable. The girls at the clerical desks, most of whom dreamed of being like Lara someday, were the first to talk about it, but the men noticed it too and exchanged glances with each other after Lara had passed.

Lara went to her office and met with Malcolm and Brenda to discuss their agenda for the days ahead; it was not uncommon for any of them to show up for work with new suggestions, for all of them kept thinking of their shared goals even when they weren't in the building, so when Lara said, "I've been thinking . . ." Malcolm and Brenda were not surprised.

But the internal qualities of that thinking, the way Lara now seemed to let thoughts develop rather than drive them forward—that did surprise them. She let her mind drift, and had they met Jones they might have recognized that the flow of Lara's mental processes matched a feeling that had begun when she and Jones were walking beneath the stars in Virginia. "It seems to me . . ." Lara went on, slowly and inwardly, "that maybe we have more resources than we know." Malcolm and Brenda glanced at each other, but Lara was not distracted by their lack of understanding—*what resources is she talking about?*—and accepted that her understanding was evolving, that it didn't have to be perfectly formed and rigid. "What I mean is, maybe instead of seeing our inability to recruit Dr. Jones as some kind of failure—which it really isn't, since if he couldn't work for us, that's not our fault or even his fault, it's just a fact—we could see it as an opportunity." Lara lifted her eyes to her friends, these people she knew—with absolutely certainty—loved her, and Lara's eyes were full of light. "I learned something from him. I learned a lot from him. He showed me his approach, and he also showed me that I could draw from that approach. We need to make modifications. We need to try again. Malcolm, I want you to go assemble the whole design team down in the lab. The Roscoes can stay the same, but we're going to change the equipment, the setting, and most of all our approach to the work. Things will be different because I'm going to be different."

"Yes, ma'am!" Malcolm said and hurried out happily.

Brenda stayed behind, staring at Lara and smiling. "Tell me about it," Brenda said. "What's changed?"

And in that moment, Lara faced the most subtle and yet most dangerous temptation; she wanted to tell

Brenda about the gift. And what would be the harm if she did tell her? Brenda was a generous and loving friend; she oversaw all of Blair Bio-Med's charitable activities. Wouldn't she be the perfect person to tell? Wouldn't she benefit from knowing the secret of giving in secret? Why not tell her?

But Lara knew immediately why not. If she told, she would be violating something: not the rule, but the spirit of the rule, the power of keeping her pride inside a prison of integrity. That's how Lara had come to think of it all: *the secret of secret giving is that it keeps your pride in prison.*

Lara just shook her head, smiled, and said, "Everything."

+ + +

They set up a new trial with the replica brain in the laboratory, and once Lara was in the hot seat, braced in a new chair of her own design, one she had fitted with fluid dampeners—shock absorbers, essentially—to try to minimize the beating of her own heart as she attempted to thread her surgical probes through the impossible passages of the practice brain, she was ready to try again. "Motion recorders ready?" she asked.

"Ready." The lead technician's voice came from the systems monitoring room, separated from the trial lab by a glass wall that insulated the surgical team from the heat and sound of the computers and tracking screens. The setup had always reminded visitors of a NASA launch, and in fact in their previous setup Blair Bio-Med utilized ten thousand times more computing power than had served the original astronauts who had walked on the moon. Now they had more than doubled that capacity; Malcolm and his teams of technicians had been busy since Lara's last attempt.

"Visual and ambient monitors ready?"

"All in sync, Dr. Blair."

"Alarms?"

"Set to 90 percent sensitivity."

"Go to a hundred."

Malcolm and Brenda stood in the systems monitoring room, watching through the glass wall. Stools waited there for them, but they did not sit. When Lara called for maximum sensitivity in the trial—eliminating all possible margin of error in her attempt before the sensors screamed FAILURE—they glanced at each other.

After a moment, the lead tech's voice came back to Lara: "We are go."

Lara reached for her instruments, only this time she was not using the same tools she had worked with before; she had ordered the exact tools she had seen at Jones's bench, the ones he used for carving his figurines. She lifted the smallest of them and began.

Sensors in Lara's instruments, lasers in the replica brain cavity, and even a grid of monitors within Roscoe, the dummy itself, measured every microscopic movement, and the bank of equipment behind Malcolm and Brenda recorded it all. Both of them found it hard to breathe. Even the technicians seemed tense, and the joke around the building had always been that the technicians would make good Roscoes because none of them had a discernible pulse.

Lara reached a critical area, the spot where she had failed in her last three attempts, and she paused. Hesitation was unlike Lara, and in the monitoring room, Malcolm whispered to Brenda, "What's she doing?"

Brenda watched Lara for a moment and whispered back, "Jones, the guy in Virginia? He told her about feeling her heartbeat. I think she's doing that."

Brenda was right. Lara was withdrawing into herself. She listened for her own heartbeat . . . became attuned to its rhythm . . . and began to move again . . .

Flanking the lead tech were four other scan specialists—it took that many to watch over the vast streams of data flooding into their computers during a lab trial, and their concentration was legendary. They could recall the readouts—numbers up to five digits—from trials they had monitored from five years before; but they never spoke, never seemed to carry any emotional investment in what was happening in the lab. Or so Malcolm believed—until he heard one of them say, "We've never been this far before."

That's when Malcolm began to hold his breath.

Lara kept going . . . deeper and deeper into the replica brain. And she too could feel the breakthrough coming . . .

Then the alarms shrieked.

The sound of the Klaxon and the flashing of the lights were even more jarring and disappointing now. They had failed again. Malcolm and Brenda felt it, the technicians felt it.

But nobody felt it as intensely as Lara. She threw down her instruments and walked out of the lab.

+ + +

She entered her office, struggling not to yell, struggling not to cry. Emotions she had contained for many years were boiling up inside her. Lara could smother an employee's despair with a single look, but her own tears were not afraid of her; as they started to come, she buried her face in her hands, then stiffened and acted as if nothing was wrong when Malcolm and Brenda arrived at her door. They entered slowly, and Malcolm said in a low voice, "We went further than ever. We won't give up. We won't ever give up."

When Lara didn't respond, he turned and walked out of the room, with as much purpose and optimism as he could manage. Brenda sat down and, with a gesture, invited Lara to talk; instead Lara stared out the window. Brenda said, "Lara, as both your corporate advisor and your personal friend, I have to ask if you're being as ruthless as you need to be here."

"Ruthless, Brenda?"

"I know you see me as a bleeding heart, but I can be quite ruthless, especially in male-female dynamics."

"Is that why you've been married four times?"

"Now *that* was ruthless. What I'm talking about is this surgeon friend of yours, in Virginia."

"He's not a friend."

"Exactly."

"What's that supposed to mean?"

"You want him to be more than a friend! And because you do, you won't push him, you won't go at him like you do anyone else who gets in the way of what you want to accomplish!"

"That's bull!"

Their voices were carrying to the secretaries in the outer office. Juliet cocked her head toward the door; two more of her secretary friends moved up to try to eavesdrop. They heard Brenda's voice rise to match Lara's: "Is it?! The big boys come at you—corporate heads, Wall Street cannibals—and sweet little Lara gets everything she wants and leaves their greedy carcasses bleeding on the floor! Now Mr. Sensitive poet-sculptor-surgeon down in Virginia says *naw* to you one time and you fly back home like a little bird. Since when did you take no for an answer?!"

"I saw he was a waste of time!" Lara responded, only slightly less loudly.

In the outer office a FedEx worker dropped off a package at Juliet's desk; she waved for him to leave it; then she noticed the package's return address.

In Lara's inner office, Brenda was exploding. "A waste of time?! Personally? Or professionally?!"

"'Personally' has got nothing to do with it!"

Brenda would not be cowed. "You've been staring out windows ever since you came back!"

Lara lowered her voice, and the secretaries in the outer office could not hear her when she said, "Brenda. You're a friend. And I know you mean well. But nothing happened in Virginia. Nothing . . . significant. To him or to—"

Juliet stuck her head in the door. "Dr. Blair—"

"We're having a discussion, Juliet!" Lara shouted.

"I know, Dr. Blair, but—"

"A private discussion!"

"I know, but—something just came for you that I thought you'd want to see right away." She put the package on Lara's desk. "It's from Virginia." Juliet drew out the name of the state: *Vir-GIN-i-a!*

Brenda gave Lara a look; and Juliet stayed put.

Lara glared at them both. "You're just gonna stand there and watch me open it?"

"Well . . . yeah!" Brenda answered, without a trace of guilt.

Lara opened the box, with Brenda and Juliet looking on; the other secretaries watched through the slot of the door.

From the protective paper, Lara pulled a tiny display case, the kind that Jones used to hold his micro sculptures.

+ + +

Lara placed the slide into the viewing slit of the microscope and dialed it into focus. Brenda and Juliet stood behind her, Brenda biting her lips and Juliet's thumbs skimming back and forth across the ends of her fingers. She had typed and texted so much in her life that emotions radiated through her fingertips.

Through the twin eyepieces of the microscope, the new sculpture became visible for Lara. She saw a remarkably graceful carving . . . And as she worked the microscope dials to shift the microscope's tray she realized it was a sculpture of a woman. She dialed again, scanning up to the face of the sculpture . . .

Lara pulled back sharply from the eyepieces.

"What?" Brenda sang, like a girl watching a favorite sister open a package on Christmas morning. "What is it?"

Lara did not answer, just stood back from the microscope, her eyes turned away and fixed on a far corner of the room, so Brenda and Juliet scrambled for a look themselves, each pulling at an eyepiece so both could view at once.

What they saw was a carving of Lara.

Jones had carved her holding a cellular phone up to her ear.

"It's you!" Juliet said, her fingertips flying in all directions at once.

Brenda said nothing; she just pulled back from the eyepiece and looked smugly at Lara.

14

JONES, FOLLOWED BY TWO young medical residents, entered Sam's hospital room, carrying the reports on all the tests Jones had ordered run on him. Jones held the folder easily in his left hand, and the ease was part of what he was teaching the students: *What is on a paper may be data, it may be scientific numbers—but it is not fact. The only fact a patient cares about is whether they are going to live through whatever has brought them to the hospital, and that fact is influenced by how much confidence they have in their doctor, so always, always stay relaxed.*

Sam was lying on his back, staring up at the ceiling, with his old buddy Allen at his bedside. When Jones entered, Allen was saying, "And since we been gone for a few days, all the fish in the lake will have got fatter, and they'll be good eatin'. That's right, Sam; that's right. We'll catch all of 'em. And the gophers will have got lazy, and we'll shoot all of 'em. Things'll be better'n ever, once we get you home."

Allen was looking up at the ceiling too, as if he could see the images of home he was projecting there for Sam. Both mountaineers turned and looked at Jones as he moved to Sam's bedside, and the residents stood respectfully behind him.

"All the tests have come back," Jones said.

"Give it to me straight," Sam said.

"You have what's called—something in Latin. It's a blockage in the main artery in your neck that feeds your brain."

Allen slapped his right hand on his own knee and said, "I knew it. He ain't been gettin' blood up there for some time."

Sam's blue eyes, watery yet sharp, snapped in Allen's direction. "I ain't been gettin' blood in a lot of places, but they ain't fell off yet."

"It will," Allen answered, "just give it time."

Jones sat down on the edge of the bed. The two residents shifted over by the window, where there sat a potted plant, grown in the window of the mountain clinic and sent down with Sam when Allen drove him down. "The blockage itself is operable," Jones said. "The odds of surviving are actually pretty good."

"There's a *but* in there someplace," Sam said, and in that moment he reminded Jones of every man he'd ever known from the mountains, the kind of men who didn't want to know how you hoped something would be, but how it was. In that moment Jones missed his father.

"Your heart's arrhythmic," Jones answered, "it doesn't beat just right. We can put you on machines for the operation, but that bounces your blood pressure, and that affects your third condition. It shows in the scans." Jones opened the folder and took out a sheet of film, holding it up to the light so Sam could see. "These thin artery walls caused your little stroke. They're ready to cause a big stroke."

"Sounds like we ought'a go down to the bank, and you take out a biiiiiig loan," Allen said, still squinting up at the ceiling even after Jones had put the film back into the folder.

"There's not much anybody can do," Jones said.

"Not much, or nothin' a'tall?" Sam demanded.

Jones put his hand on the old man's shoulder. *Always touch the patients,* he had told the residents; *people need human contact, especially when they're old, especially when they're sick. Don't just tell them you care, let them feel it.* "Let's see if medication will help."

A voice on the intercom called, "Dr. Jones, line four . . ."

Jones left the residents to confer with Sam about the medication and moved out into the hospital corridor, where he picked up a wall phone and said, "Jones."

He heard Lara say, "The cell phone was a nice touch." Her voice was softer, happier, more relaxed than he had ever heard it. He guessed that she was somewhere away from the office, because it wasn't an office voice he heard at the other end of the line. In fact she had stepped into her private apartment to make the call.

"I thought you'd like that," he said.

For a moment he heard only silence, but in that silence he heard—no, he felt, in the same way a patient felt a doctor's true caring—her smiling. Then she said, "Dr. Jones, I think we may have a solution here. We've used scans of an actual patient coupled with mapping techniques we got from NASA to construct a model brain that mirrors precisely the condition we're facing.

We call it Roscoe. Now this replica contains microscopic sensors that alert us to any mistake. You with me so far?"

"You nearly lost me at Roscoe but I think I'm muddling through."

"What if you did the operation on the model?"

"What good would it do? Even if you could duplicate my moves exactly—"

"That's just it—we can! Roscoe's sensors transmit to hard drives that collect every nuance of the surgeon's movements—and that's only half our equation. The other half is that we can replicate those movements with absolute precision."

"Roscoe must have a lot of sensors," Jones said into the phone, laughing.

"I think the scientific term for it is 'oodles,'" Lara said. "Somewhere between 'scads' and 'a truck load.'" Lara, leaning back on the white couch in her apartment in the office building, realized in that moment that she had not joked with anyone for a long, long time—for longer than she could remember. She looked out over the city beyond her windows, at the clouds above the city, at the sky above the clouds. How long had she been looking down? She ran her fingers over the silken fabric of the couch. *Who buys a white couch, anyway?* she thought. *And when did my life become so sterile?* She stood and walked to the window. "We do the operation until we get it right. Then we make our machine repeat it."

"Your machine," Jones said.

"You know that device Thomas Jefferson invented, to duplicate the motions his hand made in writing, so he could make copies of his letters? Our machine works on the same principle."

"His machine didn't work."

"Ours didn't either, at first. But now we have magic computers and space age materials, and sensors that can feel a gnat's eyelash. Roscoe isn't alive. But you are. So how about it, hotshot? How good are you?"

+ + +

It was a gray morning in Charlottesville when Jones stepped out of the cab onto the airport tarmac and carried his overnight bag to the Blair jet. A slender young woman in a white shirt with epaulets waited at the ladder. "Dr. Jones, I'm Angelica, your pilot," she said. "Since you're the only passenger you can fly in the cockpit if you'd prefer." She turned and led the way up the steps into the jet.

Jones smiled. *This is gonna be fun*, he thought.

Two minutes later he had buckled himself into the seat beside Angelica, and they were taxiing on the runway. She pushed the throttles forward and the plane accelerated with a suddenness Jones had never experienced in an aircraft. "Where'd you learn to fly, Angelica?" he asked, not with the greatest of ease.

"The navy," she said, pulling her radio headset off one ear so she could hear him better. "I flew fighters off carriers—'til I got bored." She pulled back on the controls and the plane took off, shooting almost straight up." Then she looked at Jones and grinned. "Just kidding," she said. "I used to be a receptionist." Angelica threw back her head and laughed. Jones, the doctor with the broad shoulders, gripped the leather of his armrests with hands that had turned utterly pale.

+ + +

Instead of a cab waiting at the private airport where they landed, it was a limo, long, sleek and black, stopped precisely beside the spot where the plane taxied to a halt. As the plane door opened Jones staggered out, held up by a grinning Angelica. "Thanks, Angelica," he said. "Anytime I don't like what I had for breakfast, I'll be sure to call you." He even managed a smile.

The limo driver opened its rear door for him, and as he stepped from the daylight into the softly lit passenger compartment, he found Lara. Her legs were crossed; she was wearing high heels and a cashmere overcoat. She looked more than beautiful; she looked happy. "Thank you for coming," she said.

Jones settled into the seat beside her and shrugged. "I wanted to try your jet. I've been in the market for a new one."

"When you fix Roscoe you'll be able to afford one."

"You're mighty optimistic."

"And you're mighty confident."

"I'm operating on a dummy."

"Oh, but he's a very smart dummy," Lara said, her voice musical as the limo rolled smoothly out the gate of the private airfield and the driver pointed its polished nose toward the highrise cluster of downtown Chicago. And it was not only Jones who recognized how newly happy Lara seemed; Lara herself noticed it too.

+ + +

On the way into the city they chatted easily. She asked about the clinic in the mountains, and he told her about Sam. She probed for the specifics of his condition, her questions perceptive and incisive. Jones had known already that she was extremely intelligent but he had assumed her approach to medicine would be mostly theoretical since she worked in the field of research and inventions; now he saw that her knowledge was deeply practical as well.

Once again, something about all this reminded him of someone else he had known, someone he had loved more than he loved life. When he realized that he was thinking of Faith, he grew quiet and had trouble looking directly at Lara.

The limo stopped in front of a majestic hotel. Lara said, "I picked this one for you because it's elegant and full of great history; I assumed you'd like that." As the limo driver stepped out quickly to open the door for Jones, she added, "We'll let you freshen up for a while, even work out if you want to—there's a great health club down the street. At four George will pick you up for dinner. Just you and me and two hundred of my closest friends."

Jones stepped out, then glanced at the overnight satchel he had brought and turned back to her. "All I brought was a sport coat," he said.

"You'll find a tux hanging in the closet of your hotel

room," she said. She watched him as the surprise soaked into his eyes.

"You didn't ask for my sizes," he said, biting his lower lip so he wouldn't grin too broadly.

"I assumed those too."

"You assumed a lot of things."

"Yes, I suppose I did." Then Lara spoke softly to the driver and the limo pulled away, leaving Jones smiling on the sidewalk.

In his hotel suite—it was not a room, as Lara had so casually designated it, but more of an apartment, with a sitting room complete with a wood-burning fireplace, and a bedroom attached to that—Jones found the closet, and the new tuxedo hanging there. Its fabric felt buttery against his fingers, and when he slipped the jacket on, it draped perfectly on his shoulders. He checked the label: a famous brand, made in Italy. And it had been altered to taper at his waist; he knew this for certain because no off-the-rack size had ever matched the span of his shoulders to the narrowness of his waist. Lara had not called his office to ask Janet for his sizes; Jones knew this too for certain because Janet did not know Jones's sizes; she had never seen him in anything except workout clothes and surgical gowns. Lara had appraised him, exactly, at a glance.

Hanging beside the tux was a formal shirt; on the closet floor were new shoes. Jones didn't need to try them on; he was already sure they would fit perfectly.

+ + +

Two hours later Jones, feeling somewhat more elegant and significantly more awkward than he had ever felt in his life, rode alone in the back of the limo. George had been waiting for him when he had stepped from the hotel and had told him they would be going to "The Cottage." George said nothing more after that; but as the limo rolled north along the Chicago freeways and then turned into the rolling countryside of the North Shore, along the edge of Lake Michigan, Jones saw that the driver kept glancing into the rearview mirror at him, and smiling.

Jones looked out the side window and saw that they had turned into a security entrance with a yellow drop bar that had been blocking the way, now swinging vertical and open, where a guard was waving them through. Jones looked ahead, past George through the windshield, and his eyes went wide: at the end of the long, tree-lined lane stood a three-story mansion. Its front door sat in perfect alignment with the lane, and between the lane and the door rose a pair of twin pinnacles supporting wrought iron gates permanently open to the outside; spanning the top were iron letters with the name of the estate: *Open Gates*. "So this is the *Cottage*, George?" Jones called, and he saw George grinning in the mirror. Parked in the circle surrounding the fountain that rose in front of the main door were dozens of elegant cars, mostly German. Flowers spilled from stone sconces on either side of the door. But what Jones liked best was the candles blazing in all the windows.

Car valets—young men and women in black vests with red bow ties—were parking the other cars, and one of them hurried up and opened the limo door for Jones, greeting him with, "Welcome to The Cottage." So the understatement was not only George's private joke. Jones stepped from the limousine and moved with the other arriving guests through the front door and into rooms of sixteen-foot ceilings and antique furniture pieces that rose almost high enough to touch them. He passed servants, with trays of delicacies and flutes of champagne, and gowned ladies who looked him over;

he followed the flow of the crowd out into the rear of the estate, where he found the grounds set with tables and a dance floor and orchestra arranged between the mansion and its gardens. He felt a growing discomfort, even as the novelty and excitement of the experience rose inside him.

Jones was used to having emotions that caused him to struggle. They darkened his mood when he opened his eyes in the morning, and they trudged through his brain at night, dream characters acting out dark tragedies in the ghost world behind his eyelids. But the emotions scraping in the center of his chest now were feelings he had never faced before.

He felt a rising sense that something far more than a business relationship was opening up between himself and Lara. He was already in the spiral of playing back their meeting in his mind and re-experiencing the emotions of each moment; he bounced between being sure she was intrigued by him to being just as certain that her interest was strictly professional. He knew that very game of emotional ping-pong was part of falling in love. And of course he had fallen in love before, when he had met Faith. Now she was gone, and for years, despite what his friends would tell him about time healing all wounds, he had been sure he would never again know anything that felt remotely like that kind of love.

Yet here he was, walking into this party, excited to see Lara and simultaneously telling himself that all that excitement was false, a dangerous delusion.

Still, he had told Lara about Faith; wasn't that a healthy sign? Didn't it mean that he could open up to Lara and therefore might find some sort of honest combination of his past with an unfolding present?

Then another thought hit him—a vicious, terrible thought, with the power to destroy every possibility of new love in his life: Jones wondered if he had used the tragedy of Faith's death as a way to make himself appeal to Lara's sympathies. He knew that thought was false— he *knew* it. And yet it made him resolve to say nothing more to Lara about Faith.

When he met Faith he knew the relationship was special—even in the initial stages of attraction and friendship, he sensed she was unique; she appealed to a place in his heart that no one else had ever touched, and even if their togetherness never went past that early connection he believed he was no more likely to forget her, ever, than he was to see a day when he could not recognize the melody to his favorite song.

And even when that connection continued to deepen, he did not find it easy to ask her to marry him. No, that was not quite true. Asking her was easy; it was deciding to ask her that was hard. There seemed to be so many ways to ruin a relationship. Even while in medical school, in his early twenties, he felt he had seen most of them already among his friends. The infidelities, the pride, the selfishness, the fear. And those were not just the failings of men; he knew as many stories of girlfriends and wives being unfaithful as of boyfriends and husbands cheating.

He had never betrayed a girlfriend. If he was in a relationship, he was in until he was out. Still it worried him: could he be faithful? He already believed that to betray Faith would be the worst thing he'd ever done. And what if he were to do the worst thing in the world? What if he were to fail at loving? So even after he knew he loved her, it had taken him a long time to propose.

And then she said yes.

And they had three months together before she died.

He had no sense of having in any way caused her death; his sense of guilt was not over that. Jones felt no temptation to indulge in the classic cliché of trying to make himself responsible for the fact that they were on the road that night. In every logical sense, Faith had led all those choices: she was the one who'd had the idea to found the clinic, she had made the plans to go that night, she was even driving when the accident happened. Jones felt responsible for many of the events in his life but he did not feel responsible for that.

The guilt, when it came, was about his heart—that he had not appreciated her enough, that he had been given a gift he failed to acknowledge, failed to respond to. And so it was taken back.

Lara, Jones already knew, might ask: God took it back? Or fate? Or chance?

Whatever gives gifts as big as she was, Jones thought.

+ + +

Lara owned three black formal dresses and they all looked the same; she had bought them several years apart and did not realize how each was similar to the last until she had brought the new one home and hung it in the closet next to the previous dress she had purchased in an effort to stay current. The truth was that Lara did not care about dresses; at least she had not cared until she was preparing for this evening, when she tried on each gown, one after another, until she could not remember what she had liked and what she had hated about any of them. Now she stood with Brenda and Malcolm and smiled at each guest as best she could—she had met them all at other events in the charity circuit of Chicago and recalled the names of none of them—and she watched the doors through which she knew Jones would be coming. "Quit fidgeting," Brenda hissed beside her.

"I'm not fidgeting," Lara whispered through a fixed smile.

"If you were operating on Roscoe, all the alarms would be screaming," Brenda said, speaking like a bad ventriloquist, through an even broader smile.

"Behave yourselves, ladies," Malcolm said quietly, from Lara's other shoulder. "Half of Chicago society is here."

Then Jones stepped out onto the veranda and down the stairs toward the gardens. He and Lara spotted each other at almost the same moment. Lara could hear Brenda gasp. As Jones smiled and moved toward them, Brenda coughed and said behind her hand, "He looks like James Bond! Like James Bond *ought* to look!"

"He looks just like his pictures," Malcolm said.

As Jones reached them, Lara shook his hand and said, "Brenda, Malcolm . . . meet Dr. Jones."

Jones shook Brenda's hand, and Malcolm's—and Brenda, behind Jones's back, gave Lara a bug-eyed look of joy.

+ + +

Jones's place card at dinner positioned him between Brenda and Malcolm. Lara sat opposite him; flanking her were two ladies that Lara introduced as officers of a group called Children's Charities. During dinner Jones and Lara made eye contact several times but did not converse. She ate little and smiled often, nodding as the guests praised her for her graciousness in hosting the event. After dinner one of the women who had dined next to Lara rose and moved to a podium perched on a low platform beside the main table, where she delivered a speech that ended with: ". . . And for the generosity of the Blair Foundation, we at Children's Charities extend a heartfelt thank-you to Dr. Lara Blair."

Lara rose and moved to the podium and the microphone, while everyone applauded vigorously yet politely, as they would—or so Jones thought—for someone they did not really know.

At the podium Lara said, "On behalf of everyone at Blair Bio-Med and Foundation, thank you." And that was it. She shook hands with the lady who had introduced her and handed her a check, as a group of photographers snapped pictures and everyone applauded again.

During the applause Lara looked at Jones, and this time she was not smiling at all.

An hour later the band was playing and the guests were dancing beneath the stars. Lara and Jones strolled the veranda, Lara greeting guests. "Senator, how are you?" she said to a man with waves of white hair.

"Congratulations, Lara," the senator said. "Well deserved!" As Lara introduced Jones and he and the senator shook hands, Jones noticed the polished patches of skin in front of the senator's ears and the wide-eyed stare that revealed the senator had had a face lift. Jones had never met a senator, and after ten seconds of talking with this one he did not want to meet any others.

What Jones did want to do was to talk with Lara. Lara felt this and stopped at the stone railing surrounding the veranda, to look out over the grounds stretching below and the party swirling everywhere. "You have a nice little house," he said.

"I'm not here much. It's more of a summer retreat."

"Yeah. Like my uncle Toad's Winnebago."

She laughed. "You have an Uncle Toad?"

"That's not his real name, of course, but nobody really knows his real name since everybody, even Aunt Betty, calls him Toad."

"How did—?"

"When he was a baby, so they say, he didn't crawl like normal young'uns, he scooched across the floor like a toad." He glanced at her laughing and said, "What, you don't have an Uncle Toad?"

She chuckled for a while, then said, "No, I didn't have an Uncle Toad."

"I guess guys that get called Toad live in cottages that are less than twenty thousand square feet."

She looked away and took a deep breath. Jones was sure she was thinking about her childhood. "My father bought this estate," she said. "The company keeps it now as a place for corporate retreats and intimate little gatherings like this one, to receive honors I've been awarded for having given publicly to charity." She paused, and Jones knew she had more to say so he did not rush to fill the space. Then she said, "I found out something, on my trip down to see you."

"What's that?"

"Faith was right." Lara's gaze drifted across her garden, full of the wealthiest people in Chicago. "When my father left me Blair Bio-Med, I was twenty-four years old and still in med school. In the first year I doubled the size of the research staff, and doubled it again a year later, after we pioneered seven new techniques in heart surgery and patented all the devices that made them possible. We went public last April. At the close of the first day's trading, my net worth had increased by 82 million dollars. And I give to charity because it's better than advertising, it makes my company look good, it brings us attention, contacts, investors, it makes me more money." Still not looking at him, she added, "The people I give to, they do good work . . . I'm sure they do. But I don't really see it, and I don't really feel it; I don't experience the good it does. What I do experience is that giving to the Lara Blair Foundation, and having people like the senator praise me for it, makes me feel oddly dirty."

Jones said nothing. He realized, when Lara looked at him, that he was staring at her.

"That was an interesting sculpture you sent me," she said.

"I thought you'd like it. It was to say thank you, for something that happened just after you left."

"What was that?"

"I visited Faith's grave. And then I went to bed. And slept."

Jones could not believe what he had just done; he had resolved to say nothing about Faith, and here it was, almost the first thing out of his mouth.

Their eyes held on each other.

"You wouldn't want to dance, would you?" he asked.

They walked together out into the middle of the dance floor and Lara allowed herself to settle into his arms; he embraced her lightly and they swayed to the music, and it seemed in those moments as if all the burdens both of them had felt now slid from their shoulders, and the world had grown beautiful in the glow of each other's gaze.

The next day they would do the test, with Jones operating on Roscoe.

15

THE WHOLE LAB WAS IN A STATE OF TENSION. The technicians checked and rechecked the computers and motion
recorders, and as they sat at their monitoring panels
they found their hands sweating. Lara Blair could be a
demanding boss, and many times she had hammered
into them a standard of perfection: what good would it
do them if they found a flawless surgical performance
and their instruments had failed to record it properly?
Lara did not tolerate mistakes in this room; she allowed
nothing but the best. Years ago they had brought in
other surgeons to attempt the operation on previous
Roscoes, but once Lara had discovered that none of
them were as skilled as she was, let alone better, she had

made all the subsequent attempts herself. But now, for the first time in years, she was bringing in this Dr. Jones from Virginia, a man none of them had ever heard of. They knew he had to be something special. Along with their anxiety to get everything right was their curiosity: *Just how good is this guy?*

Malcolm and Brenda were in the control room, edgy with the same question.

Jones stood in the center of all this, surrounded by fluoroscopes and magnetic resonance imagers and three-dimensional monitors and some other equipment that even he didn't know the names of. He was gowned and gloved and looked around at everything with some amusement.

Lara was beside him, making sure everything was perfect for him. When she was sure the surgical instruments were all laid out to his liking, she glanced to the glass wall and asked, "Motion recorders ready?"

"Ready," said the tech's voice, from the speaker by the glass.

"Visual and ambient monitors ready?"

"All in sync, Dr. Blair."

"And the alarms?"

Suddenly the alarms sounded and the warning lights

flashed in demonstration. It was a jarring experience, and Jones grimaced and looked at Lara. "They go off when your instruments touch any of the areas that would damage the brain," she said. "We made them unpleasant, to remind us that mistakes are lethal."

"We are all go, Dr. Blair," the lead tech said through the speaker.

Jones snapped his rubber gloves and smiled. "Let's go," he said.

Lara looked down at the replicated cranium and brain on the surgical table. "Roscoe, you ready? I guess we're all ready. Good luck." Without another look to Jones, she moved into the monitor room.

Had she looked at him, Jones might have thought she was confident; but the way she left the surgical lab told him how anxious she was about what he was attempting. And with their boss so nervous, the tension of the others in the lab—Malcolm, Brenda, the technicians leaning over the monitors and control panels—was extreme.

Jones lifted a scalpel. And dropped it. "Ow!" he shouted, hopping as if the blade had hit him in the foot, and he bumped into the instrument tray, making a slapstick clatter. Everyone in the monitoring room—

all except Lara—looked through the glass in open-mouthed horror.

But Lara was already smiling when Jones picked up the scalpel, flipped it in a rapid spin, and caught the razor-sharp instrument between two fingers. "Come on, guys, loosen up," Jones said, and as they realized he was poking fun at them, he lifted his mask, spat on the scalpel blade and wiped it on his sleeve. "Okay, Roscoe, all sterile! Here we go." He turned to the replica brain on the table and made a quick, sure incision.

From that moment on, Jones was all business. And Lara, Malcolm, Brenda, and all the others watched quietly, transfixed by the sureness of his technique. In the laboratory control room they could speak without Jones hearing; still their voices were muted, in awe. Brenda leaned close to Lara and whispered, "Why is he going so fast?"

"He's already done it in his own mind. He just lets his hands go, so his thoughts won't intrude."

They watched Jones's remarkably steady hands work their way into the crucial area of the test brain. "You guys keeping up in there?" he called.

Lara reached to the control panel in front of the lead tech and hit the talkback button. "We're hanging on.

And there's no need for you to shout. We can hear you just fine."

"I was just trying to wake Roscoe up; he seems a little unenthusiastic to me." Jones paused to look at the replica brain, then at the scans of the real brain that Roscoe was made from, displayed in high definition on a huge monitor placed at the foot of the surgical table so that Jones could see it with the slightest shift of his eyes. "Well," Jones said, "here's where we separate the men from the boys. Or the girls. That's a joke."

"Just get on with it, please. Our instruments are recording, and I'm the one who has to pay our electric bill this month."

"I'm entering the cortex."

Now all the playfulness disappeared. Jones eyes settled into a trancelike stare and he began to work the probe in minuscule movements.

On the control room's monitors the movements showed in massive magnification. One of the assistant lab techs noticed something, and wondered aloud, "He's moving like . . . in pulses."

"He moves between heartbeats," Lara said, her voice stronger than she felt.

The lead tech read his monitors, then checked them

again to be sure. "He's reached the failure point of our best attempt," he said.

Jones kept moving . . . kept moving . . . and then paused. Holding the handle of his probe absolutely motionless and moving only his lips, he said, "Show me your last trial at this section."

The techs stabbed buttons; flashing onto the screens in front of Jones were three views of Lara's last attempt—a wider view of her, a closer external view of her instruments on Roscoe, and the view of the optical fiber cameras in the simulated brain. Jones watched the replay, watched Lara's instruments trying to negotiate a turn through the same passage of synthetic blood and bone as his instruments were about to attempt. On that recording the failure lights suddenly flashed, and in the recorded replay Lara turned in frustration to glare at the camera.

"Okay," Jones said, "give me real time again."

They switched his monitors back to displaying his current attempt, and Jones drew in another long, slow breath and then continued, resuming his rhythmic, trancelike state.

In the control room they watched him breathlessly, as their monitors showed his probes working ever deeper into the replica brain.

The lead tech glanced up at Lara's back; she was motionless, staring through the glass at Jones. "We've never been this far before," the tech said.

"What's the threshold level on the death sensors?" Malcolm asked.

"Ninety-five percent of fatality level," the tech answered.

"Make it a hundred five! We're talking a human life here!" Malcolm snapped.

"I have no ego in this, Malcolm," Lara said evenly. "He's not competing with me." She turned back to the glass, stared through it for a moment and added, "It's more like he's competing with God."

Jones had reached the most critical area. Lara had never made it that far before—no surgeon ever had cut that deep, except on an autopsy. In the history of brain science it had been thought impossible for any doctor to thread surgical instruments through such critical areas of a living brain and have that brain survive. Lara Blair's father had tried for decades to do it and had failed; Lara had spent years in the same quest and had built on her father's work to go even further, but ultimately she too had reached the point where all her knowledge, all her skill, and all her hopes could not take her beyond those limits. Now Jones was standing almost within reach of what had become for Lara the Holy Grail.

Jones inserted a second tiny instrument—a wire of gold so fine that most surgeons could not even lift it without breaking it—into the channel of the first probe he had pushed into place; he paused for the space of a heartbeat and then made a move . . .

A sudden noise exploded the silence. But it was not the alarm: it was a bell, and with it, a steady green light burning above the control panel.

"What is that?" Brenda said, angry that everyone else seemed to know but she didn't.

Jones pulled down his mask and looked at Lara.

Lara began to walk, very slowly at first, across the control room, through the door into the surgical lab.

Malcolm, watching Lara, said to Brenda, "He's done it."

Lara moved into the lab, faster and faster until she was running into Jones's arms, laughing and shouting: "Yes! Yes!!!!!"

16

ONE OF THE TECHS had an old boom box in his locker, and he had placed it top of the control panel; it was blaring "Start Me Up" by the Rolling Stones. Champagne corks were popping and researchers from other parts of the company as well as executives and secretaries were joining the excitement as the celebration spilled through the rear doors of the control room and out into the hallways. Only the surgical lab itself, where Roscoe now lay with a new smile drawn on his face in Magic Marker, was off-limits. This was a day for the whole company to taste victory.

On the monitors of the control room the techs were replaying Jones's work for their fellow geeks, marveling at what he had accomplished. "Look at this margin!"

one of the techs said, over the music and the laughter. "You know how close that is to the death sensor?!"

"Two micrometers," his fellow geek said.

"Two micrometers! That's like one tenth of a human hair!" The control room was full of people hugging each other, pounding Jones on the back, congratulating Lara. She found Jones with her eyes and raised her champagne glass in toast to him; he smiled and returned the gesture.

Malcolm was in a flurry of activity, giving instructions to his aides. "I want twenty video copies of this trial overnighted to the top neurosurgeons on our list."

"The stock'll go through the roof," the aide said.

"Tell them to block out training time and give us an estimate on when they could attempt the surgery!"

As Malcolm rattled on, Brenda moved up beside Jones. "Not bad," she said. "For a poet."

"You're the corporate shrink—right?" Jones asked Brenda.

"Yeah," Brenda said. "You wanna see my couch?"

The company lawyer appeared beside Jones and said, "We have some paperwork you'll need your attorneys to look over." Lara stepped out of her crowd of well-wishers and moved toward Jones, reaching him as the lawyer was adding, "We'll have preliminary drafts delivered to your hotel. Once your attorneys get back to us and we've sorted the details—"

"We don't need to sort," Lara said. "Dr. Jones can name his price." She said it loudly enough for everyone in the room to hear.

"That's right, Dr. Jones!" one of the techs said. "Who da man? You da man!"

Jones grinned and told the tech, "Hey, good job with those monitor references."

As the tech held up his hands to the applause of his friend, Lara asked Jones, "What were you looking at there, when you paused?"

"The route you tried through the nerve bundle in the center of the cortex. The aneurism wasn't the same on my Roscoe as on yours."

Malcolm, who seemed to hear everything everybody ever said within the walls of Blair Bio-Medical, stepped closer and said, "Both replicas are made from the same patient. And we made them identical to the scans. Didn't we?"

"Absolutely," the lead tech answered. "I checked them myself."

"Then the scans were made at different times," Jones said. "Flash 'em up."

The lead tech punched two scans onto the overhead monitors. Lara moved over and compared them. Suddenly the room had gone quiet.

"He's right," Lara said into the stillness. "The aneurism on this new scan has deteriorated. Roscoe is too far behind."

The room was so quiet it was painful. "Hey, cheer up, guys!" Jones said. "Most patients don't deteriorate; until there's a sudden rupture, the anomaly is stable. Once you get production up to speed, keeping your scans up to date will be no problemo!"

Everyone waited for Lara's judgment. She was still staring at the scans . . .

But what she was really looking at was the inner turmoil she always kept from everyone else around. For a long, long moment she did not turn around; when at last she did, she smiled and looked at Jones. "Your Roscoe was even harder than mine. Today is a great victory for the company. I want to celebrate."

As the clamor around them resumed, she leaned closer and whispered to Jones, "With you."

+ + +

They rode in the backseat of the limo, a respectable distance apart. "So where do you want to go?" Lara asked.

"Where do you celebrate your victories?" Jones asked back.

Lara called to the driver, "George, see what wonders you can work."

"Yes, ma'am!"

As George raised the privacy screen and went to work with his cell phone, Jones studied Lara. "Are you bothered about the difference in the replicas? Seemed like a big deal to Malcolm."

"He's head of operations, he's a perfectionist. But there's nothing in life that's perfect, is there?" Lara said this as if she had just come to confront life's flaws for the first time, as if she had let go of something and was ready to move on. "I've looked at scans and surgical trials all my life. It's time to get on with it."

"Get on with . . . ?"

"Life."

+ + +

George seemed pleased with himself as he pulled up outside the sports arena, hopped out, and opened the door for them. "Got two seats in the owner's box!" he said proudly. "He's a friend of the senator."

Lara stepped out, and Jones was just sliding over to

get out the same door when Lara stopped, blocking the doorway. She stood staring at the parking lot, the arena, the crowds.

She stood there long enough for George to say, "Game's about to start, Dr. Blair."

Lara turned back and spoke to Jones. "Are you crazy for this game?"

Jones shrugged, noncommittal. He felt up for anything; most of all he wanted to do what she wanted to do, for he felt Lara was working something through, something private, even secret.

She turned back to her driver and said, "George, why don't you take the tickets?"

"Me . . . ?"

"And—and give one to a kid, maybe that skinny one over there. You got your cell phone? When the game's over, call a cab, on me. If you can't get a cab, take a limo." She turned and shut the door, sealing Jones in the passenger compartment, hopped behind the wheel of the limo, and pulled away.

George stood there baffled, and then he grinned and headed toward the kid selling souvenirs.

Lara swung the limo out of the parking lot and lowered the privacy screen so she could watch him through the rearview mirror. "Am I being kidnapped?" Jones asked.

"Cause trouble and I'll come back there and torture you."

Jones moved up to the rear-facing seat in the passenger compartment, just behind the privacy screen, so he could speak to her through the opening just behind her. "So where are you taking me?"

"I know just the place."

+ + +

He sat there behind her and watched her driving. She did not glance into the rearview mirror for a long time and he said nothing, and yet they both felt connected, encased together in both peace and adventure, moving into the unknown. Jones wanted to touch her, put his hand on her shoulder, or reach his fingertips into her hair, or cradle her palm into his. But he just sat with her and rode quietly.

Lara turned the limo onto the long tree-lined drive that he recognized as the lane that led to her estate. Then she looked into the rearview mirror and caught his eye. "Tonight I'm making up for lost time," she said.

She parked in the rear of the mansion, got out and

led him into the kitchen, switching on lights. "First," she said, "we eat." She opened one of the huge refrigerators and found food left over from the party.

Jones leaned against the counter behind her. "Can I help?"

"Not a chance."

A butler appeared, blinking with surprise. "Dr. Blair?"

"Oh, hi, Harold. Harold, Dr. Jones."

"Hi, Harold."

"Is there anything I can get for you?"

"Thank you, Harold, no—in fact, you and Gladys should take the night off. Come back tomorrow. Late tomorrow. Day after tomorrow."

Harold hesitated.

"Good night, Harold."

"Good night, ma'am. Dr. Jones."

"'Night, Harold."

Lara seemed dissatisfied by the contents of the first refrigerator; she opened a second huge refrigerator and found cream pastries. "Aha! We start with dessert!" She shoveled a couple of plates of pastries out to Jones and then grabbed two bottles of chilled champagne.

An hour later they were sitting in the breakfast room of the mansion and Lara was opening the second of the champagne bottles; the first was already upside down in the ice bucket. She had lit candles and put the plates of party confections on the table; now she poured herself another glass of champagne—Jones had taken only a few sips of the first glass she had poured him—and then she used her fingers to dig into a whipped-cream dessert as she kept talking with rapid excitement, exactly like a child on too much sugar. "You know I love whipped cream. And I never eat it! Is that ridiculous, or what? More champagne? You hardly touched the last bottle."

"You're trying to take advantage of me."

"Drink up, plowboy." She tipped the bottle of bubbly like she was dousing a fire, overflowing both their glasses; he clinked his glass with hers and sipped. She took a long swallow of champagne and looked out over the dark acreage of her estate. "I used to blame my parents that I was such a stick-in-the-mud. Or I blamed the company. But it wasn't everybody else, it was me." She scooped her index finger into another treat and licked it clean. "Ooo, this one's the best! You've gotta try it."

She put her finger to his mouth. When he started to lick she swiped the cream onto his nose. He lifted a hunk of pie. "That's good but you gotta taste this!" He held it out so she could take a nibble; then he smeared the pie across her mouth.

Her eyes lit up and she grabbed at a whole pie. "Food fight!" she squealed. She drew back the pie to throw and he grabbed a dessert to retaliate, when she said, "Wait!" After a pause she added, "I've got a better idea."

+ + +

The rear of the house was completely dark; then floodlights flared, switched on in stages until the entire rear garden was ablaze. The flowers and decorations still sprang fresh in their vases, and the dance floor lay clean and bare, as if the party planners had left it until daylight so that the surrounding trees could step onto it and cavort to the sound of the wind in their branches.

Lara emerged from the kitchen, carrying a boom box and leading Jones. She filled her lungs with the damp spring air and sighed, "Ah. The decorations are still in place, and the guest list is just right."

"The hostess is beautiful," Jones said, smiling.

"Let's try the band. It's from the housekeeper." She switched on the boom box and a Spanish ballad leaped from the speakers. Lara twisted the dial and began to surf the channels.

"Wait! That one!" Jones said when she dialed across a honky-tonk dance tune.

"You're kidding me."

"No! Here, do what I do!" He took her hand and led her through the simple movements of a western line dance.

Lara struggled her way into the rhythm. "This is great! How am I doing?"

"You dance like a doctor. But . . . that's a good thing!"

She switched the radio dial and found an oldie ballad.

And without embarrassment, as naturally as breathing, they began to dance, holding each other close.

Encircled within each other's arms, they felt love rising, not just its lofty emotion but its earthly, physical trance. Both of them sensed it; they broke apart immediately. Jones looked around for anything else to focus on, anything besides her *yes*, and spotted the barn. He struggled to make conversation. "That's the nicest barn I've ever seen," he said. "But I don't smell horses."

"No. They're all gone. My father built that barn."

They walked together, side by side but not touching, out of the dome of light around the gardens and into the unlit night, to the broad mouth of the barn. Lara reached for the switch on the wall and illuminated a lane of cedar chips between green- and white-painted walls, with stables carpeted in clean hay, all empty. It wasn't an extravagant showcase, it was a practical, working barn. Lara said, "He worked so hard to control life and health. He saw horses as wild and liberating."

Jones took a few steps down the lane between the horse stalls, then stopped. She watched him as he looked around, breathing in the spirit of the place. "He built this barn for you, didn't he," Jones said. Not a question but a statement.

"You know, you scare me sometimes, what you see."

"Why didn't you keep the horses?"

"It wasn't fair to them. I didn't ride them anymore. I was too much like my father, caught up so much in the future that I couldn't live now. . . . And you . . . uh . . . I just want to thank you for . . ." Suddenly she couldn't speak.

His eyes were shining. "No. I owe you," he said. "My life is in the past. I won't ever escape that. But you've given me a little piece of the present. I'm the one to thank you."

Surprised, disarmed, she smiled.

"I guess I'd better get back to my hotel," he said.

"Yes. I'll drive you."

They started toward the door, both of them sure the danger had passed.

They were wrong. Neither moved first—they reached for each other's hands—and the moment their fingertips touched it was explosive. They kissed.

In that moment Lara could feel everything she'd ever wanted to feel. Then she stopped abruptly and turned away. "I'm sorry," she said. "I'm so very sorry."

"What . . . ?"

"It's not—it's not right. I've used you. I'm sorry. I should never—" She pulled away from him; it was easy, his arms had gone numb.

"Used me? How have you—"

"I can't love you. And you can't love me. We have no future. This night was selfish of me . . . so selfish."

He tried to take her back into his arms, but she stepped completely away from him, pulling in breaths as if to sober herself from the intoxication of love, of life.

Jones stood there watching her, not hurt, not angry, just mystified. "I don't understand," he said quietly.

"I wish I didn't. I'll call you a cab." Then she hurried out, leaving him alone . . . and desolate.

17

JONES FLEW HOME ALONE.

Lara returned to her work in Chicago and spent endless hours staring blankly at new engineering plans and listening to Malcolm stalwartly trying to push ahead with their research.

But she couldn't keep from staring out the window, her mind in Virginia.

Jones, the second night after he had returned to Charlottesville, took a detour as he walked home from his shift at the Emergency Room and found himself stopped outside the restaurant where he and Lara had first tried to have dinner. He stared through the glass at the table where they sat, and he watched as the maitre d' seated a young couple at the romantic corner he and Lara had occupied, and their happiness burned Jones as he felt the loss of Lara's presence.

At the same time that Jones pulled himself away from the restaurant and walked on along the silent sidewalk, Lara stood at the veranda of her estate, looking out over the empty grounds.

+ + +

Jones pulled his car to the shoulder of the mountain road and stopped. He stepped out, careful not to make noise. He lifted a large box from the passenger seat and walked through the foggy darkness of the mountain.

He came upon a dark, silent house trailer tucked into the trees; a pickup truck sat beside it. Jones moved quietly to the bed of the pickup and left the new power saw he had bought that afternoon, down in Charlottesville.

+ + +

In the mountain clinic, Jones clipped the ends of the stitches he had sewn into the arm of a teenager who had been bow hunting when he fell from a shooting stand and impaled his own bicep. The door of the clinic opened, and Allen appeared. "Doc . . . can we talk a minute?"

Jones followed Allen outside to his rusting car; Sam sat in the passenger seat. Sam looked frail, but was in his regular overalls again. "Sam," Jones greeted him gently. "What can I do for you?"

"Operate on me."

Jones tried to find a way to respond and had no words.

Sam said, "I know. I know there ain't much hope. But that's the point." He gazed at Jones so directly, with eyes that had seen much truth and so many lies and held so much wisdom to distinguish between them, that Jones felt himself in the presence of something divine. But Sam was mortal, and that was his message. "Men like me, and Allen, and your daddy, we lived our whole lives without much hope. Can't earn a living in the mountains, people said. The mines would close, crops would die, then your children would die. And all that happened. But we went on." Sam's gray eyes scanned the gray mountains. "When your daddy died, people said you wouldn't turn out to be nothin', but look at you. A doctor."

Andrew—for he felt like a boy now, in Sam and Allen's presence, not Dr. Jones but the boy who grew in and from these mountains, looking up to the men like the one who sat in the car beside him—said, "That's all I am, a doctor. And not even a whole one."

"Boy," Sam said, "ain't nobody here impressed that you got learnin'. We're impressed you're here. You're hope to me. And a man like me, I don't need much hope. But I need a little. I'm worse than dead without it."

+ + +

The next day, Jones checked Sam into the hospital in Charlottesville and ordered a complete set of scans on his brain. When the scans were ready, he took them to his office, told Janet to hold every phone call, and began studying the scans obsessively.

He used a tiny instrument to trace a route he might follow. He paused to look at his hand. It was rock solid.

An hour later the Emergency Room nurse dropped by Jones's office; Janet looked up and said, "Everything okay?"

"Yeah," the nurse said, "I just—He's seemed especially quiet the last couple of days."

"He has, hasn't he."

"What's he doing now?" the nurse wondered, looking toward Jones's closed door. A closed door was unlike him, and Janet knew it too.

Janet leaned closer to her and whispered, "I think he might be thinking of operating again." The nurse locked eyes with Janet; both of them knew that news would spread through the whole hospital and the medical school, if it were true. "He admitted a patient from his clinic in the mountains this morning."

"He's done that before. Why do you think that means he might operate?"

"Because I peeked in on him a few minutes ago, when he hadn't made a noise in an hour. And . . ." Janet said in a whisper, "he was praying."

+ + +

Stafford, the young surgeon Jones helped worked his way through his own operating room crisis, had not believed it when Jones first told him that morning, but the look in his eyes had removed all his doubts. Stafford was still thinking about that look when a nurse moved up to him in the hallway and asked, "Is it true?"

"He's gonna do it," Stafford confirmed.

Merrill, the anesthesiologist, had just seen the operating schedule; he came around the corner, spotted Stafford and the nurse, moved up to them and said, "I don't believe it."

"I'm assisting. So are you," Stafford told him.

Then another surgical resident hurried up to them. "Did you guys hear Jones is going to operate?"

+ + +

Sam sat quietly as the surgical prep assistant ran an electric clipper from the nape of his neck all the way to his front hairline. His old friend Allen sat beside Sam and watched the process with particular interest. Allen squinted at Sam's shiny dome and said, "You look kindly like one of them fellers goin' to the 'lectric chair." Sam tried to smile.

Jones walked in, and Sam looked up. "Why do they have to shave my head for an operation on my neck?"

Jones sat down on the side of the bed. "Remember I told you about the possibility of a clot kicking loose and lodging in your brain? We have to be ready to take the clot out."

"I'll be ready," Sam said. "How about you?"

+ + +

The surgical assistants had laid the instruments out with great care, but the lead surgical nurse checked them twice, and then Stafford checked them, before

Jones entered and checked them all again. Then they wheeled Sam in for the surgery.

Jones—gowned, capped, and masked—appeared to Stafford more focused than ever as he checked all the connectors of the monitoring equipment, then glanced around at his whole team. The nurses adjusted the surgical draping, leaving the left side of Sam's neck exposed. The rest of his body, except for his head, was covered. The anesthesiologist had given Sam a Valium an hour ago to be sure he was calm; Sam had already fallen asleep when they connected the IV drip to his arm and began to administer the fluids that would keep him sedated through the whole procedure. The anesthesia medications were toxins that temporarily poisoned the body into paralysis, but they would keep him still enough for the surgery; when he came around in the recovery room he would be nauseous for a while but he would remember nothing, and blood would be flowing easily to his brain. At least that was the plan.

Jones moved closer to Sam's side and then noticed that the seats above them in the observation booth were full of his surgical students.

"Want me to get rid of them?" the head nurse asked.

"Not now," Jones said through his mask. "Let 'em stay."

He lifted the scalpel over the artery in Sam's throat. He paused.

The other doctors saw him hesitate, and they willed him on.

Jones took a deep breath and slid the blade into Sam's living tissue.

+ + +

He was not surprised when the sensations first hit him; in fact it was exactly as he expected it would be, an impact in his memory as sudden and shattering as the jolt of the truck against the car on the night Faith died. What Jones had been unable to prepare himself for was the sickness in his gut, the rising impulse to vomit.

He fought to keep his mind on what he was doing, on the sights and sounds and smells directly in front of him now, especially on the feeling in his hands; that was what he most feared losing, the Touch. But it was still there. He felt himself moving fluidly, gaining momentum.

Then as he lifted another instrument and reached again to thread instruments into Sam's carotid artery, another memory ripped through him. He felt the cold pavement under his body and the hot blood running down his face and heard voices shouting everywhere, "Get a doctor! Get a doctor!"

He almost screamed aloud, there in the operating room, *"I'm a doctor!"* And he fought the memories off, his hands staying steady, and in a firm voice he asked for tools one by one: "Probe . . . forceps . . . scissors . . ."

He worked steadily, his hands sure.

"Doing great," Stafford said beside him, sounding remarkably like Jones had sounded when Stafford needed steadying.

Then suddenly the monitors begin to ping. "His heart rate's dropping," Merrill, the anesthesiologist, said. "Blood pressure's in trouble." He rechecked his monitors and his voice took on an anxious edge, behind his mask. "He's having a heart attack. Get the paddles ready!"

Jones sped up, his movements doubling in speed. In the gallery above him, one of the surgical students leaned to another and whispered, "His hands are awesome."

The monitors were flatlining. The anesthesiologist and the head nurse readied the paddles to slam Sam's heart with the voltage that would reset his heart's electrical patterns and get it beating again.

"Done!" Jones shouted. "He's closed!"

"Clear!" the anesthesiologist called, and they shot voltage through Sam's chest.

But the monitors stayed flat.

"Again!" Jones ordered.

"Clear!" They jolted Sam again.

"Got a pulse!" the anesthesiologist said. Then he looked toward the brain activity monitor.

There was no activity at all.

Jones didn't need to look at the monitor. He already knew.

+ + +

The hospital seemed empty; it was quiet, so they say, as a morgue.

Jones sat outside the Critical Care Unit. He looked up as Stafford, on Angel of Death duty, stepped out into the hallway and moved up to him, with the decisive strides that Jones had taught him to take. "Dr. Jones," Stafford said, "we're . . . at a crossroads here. We—"

Jones looked up and nodded.

Stafford sat down next to him and said, "It had nothing to do with the operation. You worked faster and better than anyone any of us has ever seen. It just . . ."

But there was nothing left to say.

18

MALCOLM DROVE A MERCEDES, the largest sedan they made. But it was six years old. Malcolm liked grandeur, but he was frugal too—at least that was how he saw himself. But most of all he liked the daughter of his best friend; he thought of Lara as the daughter he'd never had. He steered the car into the circle in front of the mansion, stepped out, and walked in the front door as if he owned the place. In a way he did; he had convinced Lara's father to buy it, after he'd found it for him. Lara's father was as driven a workaholic as she would become, and Malcolm had hoped a beautiful home outside the city would draw both of them into a life beyond work.

Malcolm knew even then that he was wrong, but still he hoped.

Mrs. Beasely, the housekeeper, heard him come in and moved out into the foyer to meet him. "Where is she?" Malcolm asked quietly.

Mrs. Beasely turned her sad eyes to the dining room windows and the barn visible through them.

Lara sat in the loft, staring out the hay door toward the horizon. She heard Malcolm climbing up to join her and knew who it was without turning around. "I know you're not sleeping, but are you eating?" he said to her back.

Lara still stared away from him and said nothing.

"We're going out to the other surgeons again. We're going to find somebody who can do this," Malcolm insisted, as he had insisted so many times before, to Lara and to her father before her.

Still Lara didn't answer.

Malcolm's voice changed, from the tone he would take in a boardroom to the one he would have used to reassure a child at bedtime. "We haven't given up," he said again. Then he sat down beside her, like her father used to do, and put his arm around her. She leaned her head against his shoulder. And wept.

+ + +

Jones stood by Sam's bed. Sam was connected to a heart-lung machine that forced air in and out of his lungs and kept his heart beating.

Jones gripped the old man's hand; but the hand was lifeless. Jones nodded his head once.

Stafford flipped the switch. The machine stopped.

Jones squeezed Sam's hand again.

Sam's hand twitched, just once, and then went still.

+ + +

Jones, still wearing his hospital scrubs, sat alone on a park bench. Night was falling, and the sky was spitting snow, and the bleak cold made his desolation complete.

He squeezed his hands together into fists. He wanted to punch something—a wall, or himself. He wanted to break his hands—and the talent that had become for him nothing but a curse.

Two hours later he still sat on the bench, and his hands were trembling from the cold. Night had fallen fully, and alone in the frigid blackness of the night, Jones felt the anger and bitterness gnawing at him, more and more. So he stood and staggered away on frozen feet.

He walked by storefronts, past other pedestrians hurrying through the night, and he was blind to all of them. Icy rain pecked his face, and he felt nothing but his own pain.

He stopped in the light of a convenience store, out of strength, out of hope, out of purpose.

He started to walk again and nearly ran into a young mother, with her baby, entering the store. Jones didn't recognize the mother. But he recognized the coat, and then the baby. It was the one whose life he had saved.

Jones stood in the cold darkness and watched the young mother inside the convenience store. She moved to the cooler, but it wasn't beer or liquor she reached for, it was milk. On the way to the cash register she picked up cereal and a loaf of bread.

It was the most mundane of things, a woman buying food for her child. But for Jones, it was a miracle. He watched in reverence.

She finished paying and walked out, glancing up at Jones and not recognizing him.

She walked away, holding her baby close to her chest, nuzzling the infant's cheek against her own, safe and warm.

Jones watched her go.

He turned and walked in the other direction, the emotions settling like dust from an explosion inside him, his thoughts tumbling, unforced, unfocused.

And then, suddenly, he understood.

19

LARA SAT AT HER DESK, but she was not working; she stared into the distance beyond her windows, as if looking toward the future and seeing nothing there. The sound of the door opening did not cause her to stir. But when she heard nothing else she said, "Just put them on the desk, Juliet. I'll sign them later."

When she heard no movement, she turned impatiently and began to say, "Just—"

As she turned she saw Jones, clear eyed, wearing a suit and tie, immaculate, focused, handsome. Without willing herself to move, she was suddenly standing.

He said, "I couldn't figure it out, how we could be so connected, and then you could be so withdrawn. I thought it was me, the baggage I carry, the poison of having a gift I can't use. I just came to the shocking realization that All Life is not about me. This is about you. The brain Roscoe is modeled after is yours."

She brought herself to nod: *Yes.*

"How long have you known you had the condition?" he asked.

"Since Med School. My father had used his own equipment to scan me, once a year since I was a child. He told me it was to see inside my brain so he could tell if my thoughts were happy. Then he said it was to test his new machines. When I was in high school I began to suspect there was more to it. As soon as I could, I ordered a scan done, and there it was. It's what my mother died of."

"What your father invented surgeries and instruments to try to fix."

"I told you I was selfish. It's my own life I've been trying to save. And you know what's sad? I haven't had a life worth saving. I wanted to fix you—when I was the one who was broken."

They had been standing ten feet away from each other; he moved past her and sat in a chair by the window. "And now you feel doomed," he said.

She could not deny that.

He looked out at the skyline of Chicago and then turned to look at her. "You were hoping I could save you. If only I could operate again. If only I could see you as lifeless as Roscoe. Well . . . it's far too late for that. I actually . . . I tried. I operated again. On Sam. And he . . . He didn't make it."

All of this—his love for her, the truth now open between them, the news of Sam's loss and the knowledge of how much that had cost Andrew Jones—broke her free and sent her rushing to him, gripping him, pulling him into her arms, wanting to give him all the comfort of her heart.

He was emotional but wasn't weeping; he was stronger than she thought. He had a plan he had come there to tell her. "I have an idea," he said. "Something that we both need. Come back with me to Faith's clinic. Let's stop trying to save the world, or even save ourselves. Just help. One person, one at a time. Maybe that's salvation."

Then all Lara's pain and all her worry fell away, and she smiled.

THE
SURPRISE

20

IT IS THEIR PALE HUE when seen from a distance that gives the Blue Ridge Mountains their name, but from the cabin nestled among them they were the mottled brown of weathered tree trunks, the gray of ancient granite, the deep green of deciduous leaves. All these colors showed vividly around the cabin. Jones opened the door for Lara and lingered on the porch as she stepped inside.

She found a long rectangular room with a plank floor, furnished in rustic simplicity. A hickory bedstead, with its feather mattress made up with quilts, stood near the hearth. "I stay overnight here sometimes," Jones said. He pointed to the cabin's bathroom, in an enclosure of pine-finished plywood. "The tub's old, but the water's hot. This place'll be yours; I'll take the cot out in the trailer."

She set down her bag and looked around. "It's almost . . . Amish," she said.

"Mennonite carpenters built it," Jones said, smiling. "There's a community of them in the next valley, and nobody works in wood like they do. They're related to the Amish, just a little more modern."

Jones clearly loved the place and admired the men who had built it. And in fact it had been not only men; when the Mennonites had agreed to erect the cabin— donating their work because the clinic provided them emergency medical care—two gray-haired grandfathers had appeared to take measurements at the site; brown-bearded fathers had pre-cut all the wood in their home workshops and hauled it up in trucks; and then it was their sons, some of them as young as twelve years old, who had done the assembly. To most observers it was a nicely built cabin; to Jones it was a work of supreme craftsmanship. And Lara immediately spotted it as art.

"It's beautiful," she said. She stepped back out onto the porch and bathed her lungs in the mountain air, drenched with sunshine. She smiled at him, then saw one pickup, then another and another, pulling to a stop in front of the clinic trailer.

"Nell's put out the word that we're here," Jones said. "Time to get busy."

Four hours later they were still in the clinic trailer, attending to an array of coughs, sprains, cuts, and pains. Lara was bandaging a boy's arm, where she had just used four stitches to close a gash; Jones was finishing an examination of Allen, Sam's old friend. Jones told him, "Your heart's good. Even if it hurts."

"Yours too, Doc." Allen looked out the trailer window, toward the cemetery beyond the church, where Sam's grave lay beneath the red dirt, surrounded by fresh-cut wildflowers and sprigs of rhododendron that Nell had placed there that morning.

Jones nodded and touched the old farmer on the shoulder, and as Allen stood and moved away Jones looked across at Lara; she was talking happily—the boy had just told her that he had wanted to try superglue on his cut but his mama had insisted he come to the clinic—and she was glowing. She caught him looking at her and smiled back.

Nell brought up her next patient, an intensely pregnant mountain woman who held her belly and shuffled her feet, clad in slippers made of the same material as towels. "I'm Dr. Blair," Lara said, shaking her hand.

"Mavis."

"What are you, Mavis, six months along?"

"More like seven."

"When was your last doctor's visit?"

"When my last young'un was born. Six year ago. I just want to make sure this one's right."

Lara tried to keep all reaction from her face; she knew the statistics on the lack of prenatal care and its correlation to a high rate of birth defects and maternal mortality. She closed the curtains around her workspace and began an examination. After she had finished, Lara helped the deeply pregnant Mavis to her truck. A silent farmer sat at the wheel, with five children scattered like dogs around the truck bed. In fact there were four dogs with them in the bed of the pickup.

As Mavis wobbled trying to get into the door—the man in the truck did not move to help—Lara steadied her and said, "Whoa! Easy, Mavis. You're young and healthy, you'll do fine, but you ought to see a doctor every couple of weeks."

"Sure!" Mavis said. "If I could leave this brood alone all day and the crops would grow themselves."

Lara steered Mavis into the passenger seat, then fished the seat belt from between the cushions and clipped it around her. Lara looked back at the load of kids.

"You said you wanted this one to be right. Was something wrong last time?"

"Maggie," Mavis said, jerking a nod toward her youngest, a girl with blonde curls poking from beneath a hooded sweatshirt.

As Mavis's husband started the truck, Lara moved to the girl. "Hi, I'm Lara! Are you Maggie?"

The girl lifted her face. There was a hole in the middle of it. The girl had a cleft palate. Everything else about her face—her eyes, nose, ears, cheeks, and chin— were as well formed as those of her siblings, but the hole in her face was all anyone could notice.

Lara stood in silence and watched as the truck pulled away. Maggie sat in the back corner of the truck bed and did not lift her face again, even to her brothers and sisters.

+ + +

The sunset that evening turned the mountain air pink and glorious. Lara and Jones sat in rockers on the cabin porch, Lara so animated she could hardly stop talking. "—And that old lady, she just kept hugging me like I was her daughter! And that old guy—"

"Cletus?" Jones broke in, with the single word he had wedged into the conversation in the last thirty minutes.

"Cletus! That's right, Cletus! I just love the names here! Yeah, Cleee-tus! His chest has been burning for months, maybe years, and three dollars' worth of reflux medicine will make him feel like a king!"

Nell walked up from the trailer, took the tinfoil off two paper plates mounded with homemade food, and handed them up to the porch. "Eat 'em while they're hot, would'ya?" Nell said.

"Thanks, Nell."

"Ya'll be good, now." With a wink at Jones, she walked to her truck and drove away. Jones and Lara were left alone for the first time that day.

Lara waved and smiled at Nell, but her enthusiasm spilled on uninterrupted. "You know how most doctors specialize and see the same ailment over and over and over? They prescribe the same two or three drugs, they perform the same surgical procedure for their entire careers? But we get to see people, Andrew! We get to put our hands on them and they give us so much back!"

Jones nodded, rocking back and forth in the chair. In that moment he thought of Faith—and how she would have said exactly the same thing.

"But Andrew . . ." Lara said, slowing for the first time. "That girl, with the cleft palate. Did you know about her?"

"I heard about her from Nell."

"You know it's fixable, completely fixable. A forty-five-minute operation."

"Yes. But it's two days away from home, and the parents won't go. And they won't let anybody else take her. I think they're ashamed of her—and of themselves, somehow."

Lara pushed a fork into the roasted pork and green beans Nell had brought. She took a mouthful, chewed it slowly, then stopped. "We could do it here. We could make a sterile room, bring in the equipment, an anesthesiologist. I could do the surgery, and you could guide me in the art. She could be beautiful, Andrew."

He looked at her for a long time. He nodded, feeling in that moment, surrounded by the dark shoulders of the Blue Ridge Mountains, that he was in a place as sacred as . . .

As a cathedral.

As the Vatican.

As the Sistine Chapel.

Lara beamed and dug into her food.

+ + +

When night came they lit lanterns and kept rocking in their chairs on the porch, luxuriating in the peace of the mountains. Lara broke the silence. "Hey. Can you sing a hillbilly song?"

"Sure," he said. "And I'm way too smart to give you that kind of ammunition."

He stood and kissed her softly on the forehead. "They'll start coming at dawn tomorrow." He headed off toward the trailer.

She called after him. "Dr. Jones? This has been the happiest day of my life."

He smiled and walked into the darkness. She stood and moved from lantern to lantern, dialing their wicks down until their flames went out.

But then she settled back down into one of the chairs and sat rocking in the Appalachian darkness, and she thought.

21

NO ONE CAME TO THE CLINIC ON SUNDAYS unless it was an emergency, and there were no emergencies that morning so Jones left a walkie-talkie on the steps of the clinic trailer and put its mate into his pocket, and he and Lara took a walk deep into the hills. Half an hour later they found themselves standing in the middle of a footbridge of rope and wood, suspended over a gorge. A stream ran far below them; they stood suspended in the sky.

"Can you hear that?" Lara asked, tipping her head as if her ears were sniffing the faint scent of sound in the air, beyond the delicious sweetness of the stream rushing over the rocks below them and the fragrance of the birdsong from the trees on either side of the rope bridge.

"Church bells," Jones told her. "On Sundays the people up here in the mountains hold services morning and evening—and think going to a doctor on the Sabbath is a sin."

"I want to tell you something . . . and ask you something."

"Shoot."

"In the week I've been here, every day's been happier than the last. The operating room we're putting together for Mavis's daughter? I want to make it permanent. Okay?"

"Okay. Did you think I might say no?"

"That wasn't what I wanted to ask you."

"I can't operate on you."

"I don't want you to. I'm like Sam, the surgery would kill me. What I want is for you to give me now. What I mean is, give me *now*." She placed her hand over his. "I can't take away your past. I can't take Faith out of your life, or all she means to you. I don't want to. All of that is part of you. And I'm in love—with you."

It was not as if he had not known this already; but there is something about those three words, when they are said aloud. Jones couldn't take his eyes off her.

She gripped his hand tighter, and her eyes shifted toward the open mouth of the valley where the sound of the bells floated up into the wind, and the mountain village lay, and beyond that larger towns, and cities, and nations, and a vast world that went about its business and felt so important in doing it; but all that mattered to her was the truth that she had found while rocking on a cabin porch, the truth she was telling him right now. "You can't change my future. You didn't give it to me, it's not yours to change. But I have right now. I want to give my now to you. And all I want from you is for you to give me your—"

He kissed her. And he did something strange, for someone who had just realized he could love again.

He wept.

+ + +

They descended the mountainside on the same path they had taken to climb it; Jones was quiet, lost in thought. Then halfway down, at a spot where another track joined their path, he stopped and said, "This way."

She knew it was not the route they had originally followed, but she came along beside him quietly, holding his hand. They passed beneath the canopy of deep green leaves, their feet rustling through the years of fallen loam until they emerged into a clearing where an unpainted house stood, its planks weathered the same color as the tree trunks. Sitting in a rocker on the front porch was Allen. Lara was sure he had heard them coming before he had seen them, for there was no surprise in his face as he watched them move up. She was sure he had sat there for a long time. A rifle leaned against the wall behind him, but it seemed more a fixture than a weapon, bullets and gophers far from Allen's consciousness now. Tobacco juice lay in a brown crust around his lips, and the spit jar beside the curved runner of his rocker was dry too. Once the tears are past, grief is a desert.

Jones led Lara to the base of Allen's porch, and Allen nodded. It was a short nod, but it was welcoming. "Allen," Jones said, "I need to ask you a favor."

"Naw, you don't," Allen said. "You need something from me, no need to ask, just tell me."

"I want you to marry us," Jones said.

+ + +

Jones had climbed up onto the porch and whispered into Allen's ear, and Allen had nodded and answered in kind, and the two of them had whispered back and forth with Lara standing there watching, until Allen had risen and stepped into his cabin, emerging a few moments later with a battered Bible.

They walked into the woods again, taking no clear path this time, but Allen seemed sure about where he was going. A hundred yards from Allen's front porch they came to a stream where crystalline water tumbled over green rocks, and there Allen stopped and turned to them. "Bring your license?" he asked, then looked from Lara to Jones and back to Lara, staring straight into their eyes. "There it is," he said.

He did not open the Bible, but Lara had the feeling he had, in his time, performed many weddings, and Jones would tell her later that Allen was both ordained and a justice of the peace. Jones, in his whispers on the porch, had given Allen his instructions, and Allen was comfortable with the program. "Say what you need to say," he told them.

Jones took Lara's hand and said, "I will love you my whole life. And I will be with you and no other, as long I live."

It took her a moment to get her hands and her lips to move, but she gripped his hands in both of hers and said, "I will love you my whole life. And I will be with you and no other, as long as I live."

Allen looked at them both, lifted the Bible toward them, and said, "What God has joined together, let no man put asunder. Amen."

+ + +

In the glow of the cabin fireplace, they made love.

They did not hurry.

As their instincts began to scream for each other their bodies grew taut, but still their eyes were soft, and they faced each other, so that everything they did was together, and everything in their lives—the fear, the grief, the pains, the hopes, all that is sex and all that is love, came together in one moment.

22

ALL OF THEM WERE NERVOUS: the line of four children, then Mavis, then her husband, sitting in a line on the metal folding chairs against the wall in the clinic trailer. Mavis took her husband's hand and squeezed it tight, until the tips of his fingers glowed red as fresh strawberries. She kept glancing toward the new operating room, visible through the trailer window.

The new operating room stood in what was just another kind of trailer, a long wooden box towed in on wheels and set up on a freshly poured concrete pad. It was a bit makeshift, but the equipment was state-of-the-art and the accessories immaculate. Maggie, Mavis's fifth child, the girl with the cleft palate, lay on the table, looking up at Lara, and Jones, and the two surgical nurses they'd brought up from Charlottesville. Maggie's eyes were blue, and they had fear in them, holding on the only uncovered human features she could, the eyes of the surgeons and nurses visible between their caps and masks. But Lara was sure she could see trust in Maggie's eyes too, a recognition from somewhere beyond thought that the woman who was looking down at her now, the same woman who had spoken to her when she was in the back of the truck, was someone who brought a gift. Maggie's parents had told her the doctors were going to make her "all better." Maggie did not fully understand what that meant. She had never known a world in which people could look at her without something terrible happening on their faces, something that said: *Go away; I would rather you did not exist at all.*

Merrill, the anesthesiologist, who said he'd donate his time the moment they told him what they were doing, fed liquid through Maggie's IV drip, and Lara lowered her face closer to the girl and said, "Just close your eyes, honey, and we'll take care of you." Maggie sank into a motionless slumber. Lara looked across at Jones, and they began.

Lara's hands, from the first lift of the instruments, moved in a fluid ballet, her eyes intense and brilliant above her mask, never looking away from the task, yet tuned into Jones's voice as he watched and spoke soft directions for the artistic shaping of the tissue. It was Jones, not Lara, who had to struggle to stay centered on the task; he had never seen her operate before, and her virtuosity both surprised and distracted him.

The time flowed as smoothly as Lara's movements; even as focused as she was, when every fragment of the experience was burning itself into her memory, it seemed over almost as soon as it had begun. They wheeled the girl into their small recovery room at the other end of their new trailer, and as soon as she awoke Lara lifted her in her arms and carried her through the connecting hallway the Mennonites had just constructed and into the waiting room, where Mavis and her husband looked up and Lara placed Maggie into her father's arms. He pulled back the covering from his daughter's face, and he and Mavis froze.

When they looked up again at Lara, their eyes were full of awe.

+ + +

A low fire glowed in the cabin's fireplace, scattering light across the rough sawn planks of the floor. Steam rose from the bathtub, where the water still sat because Lara had just been reaching to pull out the stopper when Jones had picked her up, towel and all, and carried her to the bed.

Now Lara lay as limp on the bed as the damp towel lay on the floor, her head on Andrew's chest, her eyes dreamy as he traced his fingertips across the landscape of her back. "Tired?" he whispered.

"When was the last time I told you this has been the happiest day of my life?"

"Yesterday. And the day before that. And the day before that." He loved the texture of her skin, and the thought floated through his mind that there is nothing in the world like the feeling of a woman's back when she is dozing in the arms of a man she knows loves her.

"Mmm . . ." she moaned. "You do have incredible hands." She moved her cheek as if to snuggle deeper into his chest—but felt the shudder go through him, like a chill through his soul. She lifted her head. "What? What is it?"

"Nothing, I—"

"Andrew . . . ?" Her eyes were open now, wide awake.

"That . . . that was something Faith said to me." He kept his arms around her, but now his fingers felt like peeled carrots, left too long out of the refrigerator.

"Andrew. Don't do that; you do-not-do-that! Don't go to the past, you are not responsible for it. It's not your fault, it's not yours to change!" He tried to look away, and she wouldn't let him. "Please look at me." She tugged his chin until he looked in her direction. "I swore I'd never say this, but I have to. You didn't kill Faith, you didn't let her die, you did your best, and it wasn't up to you. Good as you are, it was not up to you. And neither is the future. It's not your fault, and it's not yours to change either. Be here, with me, now. *Be here, with me, now—*"

She was kissing him, willing him to her with all her heart, wanting to heal him not with her skill or her knowledge, but with her love.

There are times in life when physical excitement swirls in the wake of fantasy or flirtation and slides in on the wave of a mighty mood, crashing and breaking and meaning no more than the breaking bubbles of sea foam that other waves leave behind.

There are other times when intimacy rises like heat from the dark core of the earth, becoming fire in the surface air, hot enough to turn ancient stone into flowing magma, leaving behind mountains, islands, continents. What happened between Andrew and Lara then was that kind.

23

IN SIX WEEKS, work was going on everywhere on the mountain. Carpenters were tearing away rotten boards from the old barn just up the road from the clinic and re-siding it with new timber; painters were at work on the house; surveyors were sighting, marking, driving stakes, laying out areas for the new construction. Nell had organized the country women into a cook crew, and their grandsons and nephews were setting up picnic tables for the food Nell's sisters were roasting on outdoor fires. Jones, standing in the center of a grid of stakes and string, heard a truck pull up and looked to see Carl arrive with his family. The children ran to the play area; his wife kissed him and joined the cooking party.

Jones watched as Carl moved to the rear of his truck and began to take out his carpentry tools. He glanced up to see Jones. Carl stopped what he was doing and said, "Oh. Hi, Doc. Look, uh . . . I know the stuff about the virus was bull. But it made me think." Jones nodded. Carl touched his index finger to his cap in a salute to Jones, then lifted his new saw from the back of his pickup and headed toward the barn to join the work there.

"Doctor Jones!" Nell called. Coming up the road was another pickup truck, carrying Mavis and her family.

"Get Lara," Jones said, and Nell ran to fetch Lara from the examination room. In a moment Lara stepped out into the sunshine, then walked up to stand beside Jones. Everyone—the surveyors, the carpenters, the women setting up the food at the picnic tables—stopped working and turned to watch. The truck tires crunched into the new gravel at the clinic turn-in, and the engine clattered to silence. The driver's door squeaked open and Larry stepped out. The passenger side opened and Mavis stepped out too. And then, behind her, came Maggie. The hole was gone now, and in its place was nothing more than a faint line on a luminously beautiful face.

For a moment everyone was silent. And then they were cheering. Maggie, not knowing quite what to do, stood beside her mother gripping her skirt until Mavis leaned down and told her it was all right to go to Lara; then Maggie ran to her and kissed her, then ran back to her mother.

It took a moment for Lara to speak. When she did her voice was husky. "I've got to get the camera," she said to Jones.

"Yeah, you do that," he said. He stood and watched it all, the happiness of the people, the congratulations of the farmers and carpenters to Mavis's family. It would be easy for an outsider—a member of Lara's management team from Chicago, for example, or even one of the medical school doctors from Charlottesville, less than a hundred miles away—to see the mountain people as one uniform society, but there were rankings among them as distinct as the social pecking order among socialites at a Manhattan soiree; the mountaineers, like the Manhattanites, knew who made money, knew who cheated on their spouse and who was faithful, knew who had children who were achieving something the others found admirable; in one place that achievement might be acceptance into an Ivy League school and in another it might be a Medal of Honor, but both recognized rank and that ranking created barriers. But as Jones's eyes followed Maggie, and the way everyone around her took in her transformation and felt themselves somehow a part of the wretchedness of her previous rejection and the grace of her newness, all their separation fell away. In that moment, they were a family.

Then Jones heard a faint crash in the cabin, what he immediately knew was the sound of a camera lens breaking. Then he heard a wooden chair knocked over onto the plank floorboards.

He ran to the cabin door and was the first one inside. He found Lara staggering, her left arm dangling lifeless at her side; before he could reach her, her legs buckled and she stumbled to her knees, falling sideways as her right leg fought to stay straight and her left gave way completely.

+ + +

Carl drove them in his pickup down to Charlottesville; Jones refused to wait for an ambulance and was too shaken to drive himself; Nell found it striking that he knew Carl would be the safest of all at the wheel.

In two hours Lara was in a hospital bed. She was

sitting up and seemed fine when Jones walked in with a folder full of test results and scans. "You shouldn't have brought me here," she said, before he could tell her anything. "We should've stayed at the clinic."

"We don't have cerebral scanning equipment at the clinic. How do you feel?"

"Normal. Ischemic attack, right?"

"Yeah. There was a swelling around the aneurism, but no rupture." He showed her the scan so she could see for herself. "The increased blood volume in your body is putting pressure on the weak vein wall."

"Increased . . . ?"

"You're pregnant."

She nodded, oddly contained and silent.

"You're not surprised," Jones said.

"I'm a doctor, and a woman. Something was different. I'd even started thinking I might make it all the way to motherhood because pregnancy does things to a woman's body, it makes her stronger and more resilient. And what a gift it would be if you and I, without meaning to, had made something more miraculous than anything our minds and our talent could ever invent."

For any other patient, Jones would have sat beside the bed; now he began to pace. The emotions rising in him were like thunderheads colliding in the sky, certain to bring a storm. "The pregnancy isn't having that effect," he said, almost angrily. "The pressure on the aneurism is going to make it rupture."

"How can you know?"

"I know because of what just happened, and you know it too. You're not going to make it to term."

"Andrew, look at me. Look at me! I won't end this pregnancy."

He moved over and sat down beside her, taking her into his arms. The rage had already passed through him, or maybe it was only the calm before the torrent, but his voice was still and calm as he said, "I know."

24

THE BOARDROOM AT BLAIR BIO-MEDICAL could have held far more people, and yet it seemed full with Malcolm, Brenda, and the company lawyer gathered on one side of the conference table and Jones seated on the other. Lara sat at the head, in the chair of the board director. "This," she began, "is no time to leave things unsaid. You three in my company have known what no one else has. And now I need to clear up what will happen when I'm gone."

Brenda was already crying and shaking her head as if to rebuke reality so sternly that it would cease to be the truth; so Lara repeated, gently and firmly, "When I'm gone. Malcolm will run the company, with Brenda in expanded duties. My stock will be in a shared trust—administered by Malcolm, Brenda, and Dr. Andrew Jones. All profits and capital value from my stock will accrue to the Blair Foundation, with this change: All gifts will be made anonymously."

She looked around the table. "That's all. Malcolm, you're in charge as of right now."

Malcolm had to take a moment to find his voice, and when he found it he had to clear it. "Where will you be?"

"There's a little clinic in the mountains that needs an extra doctor. I'm going to go back there and look at every day as a day I'm living, not as a day I'm dying."

Malcolm, Brenda, and even the company attorney were all having the same experience; each felt the moment in their own way, of course, but all of them floated in a sea of sadness and defeat.

But to Jones the moment was somewhat different; he felt torn. He felt as if there was something he should do, if only he could do it. As the others sat across the table from him and wept, Jones secretly slipped something from the inner fold of his wallet and glanced down at it.

It was the old postcard of Creation—wrinkled and stained.

Lara took a long and shaky breath. "This isn't a time to leave things unsaid. I love you all."

She stood and left the room.

Jones looked at their tearful faces across the table from him, and then he stood and followed Lara.

+ + +

He caught up with her at the far end of the hallway. She stopped, turned to him, and whispered, "I'm so sorry, Andrew. I told you I wanted to give you my now. I didn't know now would be so hard."

He said, quietly but firmly, "If I could have a child who's part of you, I'd be grateful for every breath I took. Either way, I'll have you with me every day I live, no matter where you are."

She thought she had steeled herself against any more tears, but they welled into her eyes now.

"It's all right if you cry," he told her.

She said, "I have to tell you the truth; I've never been able to tell you anything but the truth. I wanted this baby. In whatever way I knew how to pray, I prayed for it. I didn't want a baby just for me. I wanted someone to love you the rest of your life, the way you deserve to be loved."

They didn't embrace; they didn't have to.

Jones said, "There's a hospital down the block. And any equipment you have here could be transferred there, right?"

"No, Andrew. No. You can't try to change this. I can't leave you with that."

"And would you have me live the rest of my life knowing that no one else could save you, and I didn't try? You were right about Faith. I did my best. I did all I could do. You're carrying our baby. You have to let me try."

And she knew he was right.

25

ONCE THEY HAD MADE THEIR DECISION, they wasted no time; there was no time to waste. They made their preparations, fired by an ever growing sense of urgency. Lara's group found a brand-new surgical suite in a hospital two blocks from their building and began to outfit it right away with gear from the Blair labs. The transporting, installing, and testing went on around the clock, and because the word of what they were doing and whom they were doing it for had spread quickly, not even the teamsters asked for overtime.

Malcolm and Brenda saw to it that Lara checked into the hospital with the attitude of a patient, not a physician, for doctors are notoriously bad patients. Brenda stayed with her constantly, obsessing about Lara's diet, rest, pre-op medications, and even the amount of light coming through the windows. Part of Jones's idea in allowing this was that if Brenda complained enough, Lara would keep insisting that everything was okay. The other part of the idea was that Brenda couldn't help herself, and if she stayed with Lara and saw to her perfect preparation, then Brenda couldn't interfere anywhere else.

Jones made his phone calls, and Angelica flew in his best team—Stafford, Merrill, and the two surgical nurses who assisted them in Virginia. Even before he let them check into their hotel rooms, Jones took them to the hospital and showed them the operating room setup, with Malcolm there with them to calm his own fears in turning Lara over to a group he didn't know. The newcomers, compulsive perfectionists by profession, frowned at the unfamiliar equipment surrounding them, but Jones calmed their concerns. "It's all for monitoring and reference, pure and simple," he told them. "Everything else is the same."

Jones's team took it all in. "Is there anything else you need?" Malcolm asked.

None of them could think of anything additional they could possibly need; the room was already packed.

Malcolm took a deep breath, and then, as hard as it was for him, he left the OR and headed back to Lara's room, where he found it necessary to stave off the impending mutiny of the hospital's regular nursing staff, who were all threatening to resign if Brenda was allowed to keep prowling unmuzzled.

Jones gathered his friends around him; he had e-mailed them the basics of the procedure they were about to perform and had made sure the plane carried a complete set of scans and even a video monitor so that on the flight up they could study his trial run on Roscoe. He knew they were aware of everything of a technical nature that they could possibly need to know. Still, he waited for them to ask any questions they might have. They were silent.

Jones said, "If the aneurism bleeds before we can close it off, we induce coma, to shut the brain down until it can heal. We're not gonna let her die on the table. We are NOT going to let her die. Everyone understand?"

They did.

+ + +

A nurse shaved Lara's head. She sat motionless as the locks fell off. She had thought that this would bother her more than anything else about the surgical preparation, but she was wrong; all of it seemed the same. As much concern as she had around her, as many people who cared, no one could take her place; she was alone now.

+ + +

The operating room at the Chicago hospital down the street from her building had become a replica of the Blair Bio-Med lab, and technicians were in place at all the monitors behind the glass separation wall they had installed overnight. Lasers and reference cameras were aimed all over the surgical area; the tools—saws, drills, expanders, forceps, and the finer instruments too— were arranged beside the table. But there was no Roscoe now. And as yet there was no surgeon.

The University of Virginia surgical group was in the prep room, scrubbed up and waiting like a team before a championship match; but Jones was not there.

In the corridor outside the OR, Malcolm kept checking his watch. Brenda walked up, pale. "I've checked the doctor's lounge, the chapel, even called his hotel," she said. "Where is he?"

Malcolm shook his head. "He walked through about ten minutes ago, looked into the surgical room, then walked out the front door. Said he needed some air. He must have—"

Brenda put an arm on his shoulder to stop him, as nurses pushed Lara, now on a gurney, toward the surgical holding room. As Lara passed Malcolm and Brenda she looked up at them and said, "He'll be here."

But Malcolm wasn't sure; neither was Brenda.

+ + +

While Lara lay on the gurney in the surgical holding room, and Malcolm and Brenda paced in the corridor, and the surgical team from Virginia checked the clock on the wall of the operating room, Jones walked the streets outside the Blair Bio-Med Building. He wandered, with no thought of where he was. Churning. Lost. Utterly alone.

He saw, across the street from the pub, an old and dingy cathedral.

Jones walked in. He moved slowly. Candles burned in the votive boxes, brightening the shadowy corners of the old sanctuary. A few people were scattered around praying, as well as a wino or two, asleep on the pews.

Jones took a seat in a pew, near the middle of the church. And he tried to pray. But he couldn't. He could not connect, could not feel a part of this place, could not find a channel to God. He gripped the back of the pew in front of him in frustration.

For the first time in his life, he felt his hands trembling.

Sitting not far from him was a gray-haired man in a worn black coat and a frayed white clerical collar. He was kneeling in prayer; he noticed Jones.

As Jones hung his head, the old priest moved over and sat beside him. "Are you in trouble?" the old priest asked.

"I think you could say that."

"Do you want to pray?"

"I can't connect, I can't pray . . ."

"Then I will pray for you. What do you need?"

"A miracle," Jones told him, as honest as he had ever been.

The priest reached into his robes for a pack of cigarettes. He lit one, right there in the old cathedral, and offered the pack to Jones. Jones declined.

"Good for you. I'm quitting—have been for sixty years. So . . . you need a miracle." He took a long drag on the cigarette, blew smoke up toward the gothic arches of the ceiling high above them, and nodded his head. "Want to hear mine?"

Jones didn't answer, but the priest went on anyway. "I have been a priest for fifty-seven years. I've seen this parish go from the center of the community, where the rich and powerful came to worship, to the fringes. Did you know that Jesus was crucified at a garbage dump?"

"No, I didn't know that." Jones knew it was called Golgotha, but if they had told him in Sunday school that it was a garbage dump, Jones had forgotten it.

The priest shrugged. "I thought that was interesting. Anyway, as this church grew less important to the community, I grew less important to myself. They didn't value me, and I ceased to love them. I can tell you truly that for the last twenty years, I have felt no love at all. And I could not remember my last honest prayer, when I had a connection. Until just a few weeks ago."

Now the priest stopped and waited. Waited until Jones gave him a look to tell him to finish his story and go away. "I was collecting from the poor box," the priest said. "The few coins that people toss in, most of them trying to buy luck, I imagine. But on this day I found a large envelope, full of money. More money than I had ever seen, certainly more than I ever held. No name. No note—except the words *For the Poor* on the envelope. I went back to my room and counted it.

It was a million dollars." He took another drag from his cigarette. "I took it to the bank, and they said it was real, not counterfeit. I called the police to find out if some amount like that had been stolen recently, but they knew of nothing. Somehow I was already sure it wasn't stolen. That it really was intended for the poor." He looked at Jones. "I see I have your attention now."

"So the money was your miracle," Jones asked, only half certainly.

"No. The money was the miracle for the poor. My miracle was what that act of charity did to me. Someone, capable enough in the ways of the world to have such a sum, decided that the best way they could think of to pass their charity to the poor was to hand it . . . to me. Why? Did they choose what was nearby? Comfortable? Convenient? Who knows? They chose. And suddenly my life was not wasted. Suddenly I was a priest again. I could pray. For them." He glanced around at the poor, scattered here and there in cathedral. Then he looked back at Jones. "And for you."

The priest looked up at the stained glass windows, darkened by decades of airborne grime. He looked at the cross above the altar. Then once again he looked at Jones and said, "You offer your hand to God. Whether

He uses it—whether your hand becomes His hand—is up to Him."

+ + +

All the Blair Bio-Med equipment was switched on and fully functional, the beams of lasers criss-crossing through the air, the sensors ready to feed data to the computers and screens in the newly connected monitoring room, where the technicians sat, their eyes reflecting the glow of the pixels.

Only this time the patient was not made of molded polymers. She was a young woman of flesh and blood and spirit, Lara Blair, lying on her back on the padded table. Jones moved to her. Her eyes were half-open, dreamy.

Jones looked at the anesthesiologist, Merrill. "Ready?" Merrill nodded. Hearing Jones's voice, Lara whispered, "Jones . . . ?" He leaned to her, putting his ear close to her lips. "This is not a drill," she said. Then she reached up, squeezed his hand, and closed her eyes.

26

JONES LIFTED A SURGICAL SAW AND BEGAN.

Tears rolled down Brenda's face, and sweat rolled down the faces of the technicians. Lara, sedated and strapped down so firmly that there was no chance of movement, lay like a corpse. Malcolm trembled. But Jones did not. His hands were sure, as he kept going, deeper, deeper . . .

Then he too began to sweat, as he reached the first stage where the slightest wrong movement would kill her. He paused; he heard the monitor beeping with the beating of Lara's heart, and he felt the beating of his own. He willed them to beat together, almost as one.

And then the memories began to hit him. He saw

blood dripping into his eyes as he staggered across the pavement and heard voices shouting, *"Get a doctor! Get a doctor!"*

"I'm a doctor!" he heard in his memory and almost shouted it in the operating room now. But what had happened with Sam had prepared him for this; he had known the memories would come, had known that they had the power to torture his soul but did not have the power to move his hand. He also knew that *he* did not have the power to move his own hand.

Before he had left the church, he had offered his hand to God.

The Blair team had calculated that it would take more than two hours for him to weave the probes through the labyrinth of critical nerve fibers bundled in the central cortex of Lara's brain; Jones was there in thirty minutes. They were astonished at his pace and might have panicked had they not been so surprised. But Jones's hands seemed to flow, though their movements to the naked eye were imperceptible; it was the data rolling from the computers onto the monitor screens that showed his probes moving deeper, ever deeper into Lara's brain.

Jones did not mean to hurry, but he knew that he could not hold back either; the stem of the brain where he was working contained the physical mechanisms that controlled all the essential functions of Lara's body, and the tiniest disruption in that area could cause the shutdown of any of those systems—or of every one of them; that is to say, death.

Now he reached the most critical area: the monitors showed it; the technicians knew it. Jones paused again, and in that pause the nightmares kept coming, the horrific scenes of the accident flashing through his own brain just as his instruments penetrated hers, as he struggled to keep his hands still and his pounding heart steady. The memories came faster and faster, with more intensity.

He looked down at Lara. Not at her brain, but at her, her closed eyes, above the mask that held the tubes that fed oxygen into her lungs. Breath. Life.

In the monitoring cubicle next to the operating room, everyone was breathless; they knew he had stopped because he had reached the double aneurism and was at the point when he must perform the most critical movement, and do it now. "Make the clip," Malcolm muttered under his breath. "Make the clip . . ."

Brenda and the technicians too began mouthing the words in a soundless chant.

Around the surgical table the other surgeons could do nothing; they knew this was it; they tried to will Jones forward. Merrill looked up from his readouts and said, "Her blood pressuring is falling. Dr. Jones? Her blood pressure . . ." After another moment he said, "Andrew . . . ?"

Jones was motionless; his mind was flashing back to Faith, dangling upside down in the wreckage of their jeep, opening her eyes to look at him.

He fought to keep the image away.

It was a fight he could not win.

So he let the memories come. And in his flashback he saw something that did not happen in the actual event: he saw Faith smile at him.

Inside the central monitor room, the equipment emitted a high-pitched, steady sound. Jones heard the monitors shrieking and glanced up for the first time since the operation began; through the glass window he saw Malcolm, Brenda, and all the others, feeling the cold grip of Lara's imminent death.

Jones made the clip, and just for a moment all the world went black.

27

THE CHURCH IN CHARLOTTESVILLE WAS QUIET. Brenda sat with tears falling from her eyes, pressing a hand to her quivering lips to hold back her emotion. Malcolm, his face dead still, sat with eyes rimmed with tears. Nell had driven down from the mountains with the others from the clinic, and she sat crying in silence. Luca had flown all night from Rome and leaned forward in the pew, his head lowered, his heart to God.

Mavis was there, with her husband and their daughter, her face now beautiful, her eyes full of tears.

Lara stood there in her wedding dress, and Andrew Jones stood beside her as the minister said, "I now pronounce you man and wife!"

The congregation erupted, and the organist played Beethoven's "Ode to Joy."

+ + +

Summer had settled fully on the Blue Ridge. The grass was lush and the clinic was blooming like the wildflowers on the mountainsides. Children cavorted on the swing sets and playground equipment around the barn. And in a rocking chair on the porch of the farmhouse, Lara finished nursing a baby. It was hard to tell which of them, mother or child, was more full of life. "There's Daddy," Lara said. "Let's go say hello."

Lara walked with the swaddled baby over to Jones, who was at the side of the barn, assisted by the surgical staff from the University Hospital, all of them in their work clothes, carefully painting the barn's broadest wall. Jones saw them coming and moved to meet them. He watched Lara's face as she took in the picture they'd been painting on the barn.

"There's something I've meant to ask you," he said. "When did you put the money into the poor box of the church down the street from your building?"

"What church?" Lara said without looking at him. She smiled and handed him the baby.

Andrew Jones looked down at his daughter. "Faith," he said, "how do you like the artwork?" He turned the infant so that she could see, with her father and mother, what the clinic's staff and the mountain people were painting on the side of the barn.

It was a copy of Michelangelo's Creation. It was a crude replica, painted with the kind of brushes people use for barns and houses, not for masterpieces. But it was a masterpiece all the same.

In its center was The Touch between divinity and humanity, between God and His creation.

An Interview with the Author

You are probably best known for writing *Braveheart*. We understand that this screenplay came out of a low point in your life. Can you tell us about that?

By the mid-1980s, I felt like my life was really starting to go well. I'd gotten married, we had two beautiful sons, and I'd won a multiyear contract with a thriving television company. Not too long after my second son was born, we bought a new home, and then six months later, the Writers Guild went on strike, which caused the company I worked for to void its contract with me. The strike went on forever, and when it was over, the company was barely there anymore. I was out of work, my savings were gone, and no one would return my phone calls.

I kept trying, of course; I was always good at trying. But one day I was sitting at home, at my desk, staring at nothing, my stomach in a knot, my hands trembling, and I realized I was breaking down. I feared I was failing my family; my greatest fear was that I would fail my sons. I was afraid they would see me come apart, and it would be something they could never forget.

I got down on my knees; I had nowhere else to go. And I prayed a simple prayer. I said, "Lord, all I care about right now are those two boys. And maybe they don't need to grow up in a house with a tennis court and a swimming pool. Maybe they need a little house with one bathroom—or no bathrooms at all. Maybe they need to see what a man does when he gets knocked down, the way my father showed me. But I pray, if I go down, let me go down not on my knees, but with my flag flying."

And I got up, and I began to write the words that led me to *Braveheart*.

This book is very different from some of the screenplays you've written—*Braveheart*, *We Were Soldiers*. Are there certain themes that run through all your stories?

Above all, I think the central theme of all my stories is that hope matters, that courage works, that love prevails. All my life, I have been intrigued by the mechanism and the moment of transformation: What happens when what we call a miracle occurs? What happens when someone does something that no one else has ever done or that they themself have never done? What happens when someone stops doubting and starts believing?

Talk about the heroes in your stories.

The heroes in my stories are fighting monumental battles—the ones that are worth their blood—and we get to see what they're willing to die for.

How does your Christian worldview impact the stories you tell?

I'm not trying to use my stories to convince someone else to share my understanding. My understanding is limited. What I want to share is my experience that hope matters, that courage works, that love prevails.

Being a Christian doesn't tip the scales one way or the other; people want a good story. I've always said that my inspiration for *Braveheart* was the New Testament, but biblical parallels aside, it stands on its own as a story. So often the term "Christian film" is synonymous with mediocrity because people ignore the fact that a story needs to entertain, not preach. *The Touch* carries a message, not a dogma.

You've been involved in many great films. What made you decide to write a book?

When I graduated, I didn't want to be a doctor or a lawyer; I wanted to be a writer. I wanted to tell the kind of stories that would let a young man know who his ancestors were, who he might be. The kind of stories that might keep a child alive through a long night.

I had my embarrassments and my setbacks, but I kept writing. Eventually I moved to Los Angeles, but it took a long time for me to really break through as a writer. I wrote songs, short stories, and screenplays.

This is my eighth book. I wrote and published four novels before I ever sold a screenplay, and my original films have always had a companion book. I've never followed the Hollywood practice of using outside writers to novelize my screenplays; I've always written the novel version myself as a way to expand the story beyond what a movie can tell in two hours.

Where did you get the idea for *The Touch*? What is your process for new story ideas? A flash of insight? A snippet of conversation? Inspiration from travel?

I've always been intrigued by the idea of secret giving. My inspiration for stories comes from my personal experiences and fascinations.

In this story, Faith leaves behind a legacy of "secret giving." Where did that concept come from? Is there a connection here to your work with Habitat for Humanity?

Certainly Jesus originated the message in His parables about giving and in His opposition to pride and public righteousness. Lloyd C. Douglas inspired me with *Magnificent Obsession*, his novel that became one of my mother's favorite movies.

Miracles are, by definition, beyond our control, but giving in secret opens us to miraculous possibilities.

Habitat for Humanity is a perpetual-motion miracle, and the people who work with it and gain homes through it have given me far more than I have given them. With Habitat for Humanity, your hands get dirty and your heart gets clean.

What do you want your readers to take away from this story?

I want readers to come away more open to miraculous possibilities, feeling in touch with the source of miracles.

How did you research the medical aspects of this story?

I wrote the story first and then went back to research to see if what I'd postulated was actually possible. A quick check of the Internet will tell you that robotic surgery is at the forefront of medical technology. Regarding the double aneurism, I needed something that had confounded doctors to set as the obstacle, and this condition seemed particularly difficult to cure.

In the story, Andrew makes microscopic sculptures. Where did you come up with this idea?

Decades ago I came across an article about a man who made carvings so small you'd need a microscope to view them, and when I began writing *The Touch*, I remembered this amazing talent.

Why did you decide to set this story in the South?

I was born in Jackson, Tennessee, lived in Memphis as a child, and spent my teenage years in Lynchburg, Virginia. The University of Virginia and rural Appalachia are familiar settings and seemed the perfect locations for this story.

You once said nothing can move an audience unless it moves you first. Is this true of *The Touch*? In what way did it move you?

The Touch is sparse, plain, direct, like the people of the Blue Ridge Mountains! I also wanted it to feel poetic, like the words of a hymn. When I read it, I feel what I felt when I sang the songs at revivals, standing next to my grandmother.

Discussion Questions

1. The story begins in the Sistine Chapel. In what ways is the famous painting *The Creation of Adam* woven through the story? Andrew's *touch* is evident in his surgical ability. In what way does Faith have the *touch*? How is it different from Andrew's?

2. Andrew carries on Faith's legacy of secret giving. How does it help him after losing Faith? Has anyone in your life passed on a legacy that you've been able to keep alive?

3. Why is it important that the giving remain secret? In what ways does secret giving affect the giver? The receiver?

4. How does that idea of giving in secret contrast with what Lara experiences when working with donors and attending fund-raisers?

5. The young Andrew Jones suffered from asthma. How does he use what he learned from that illness to perfect his surgical procedures and make microscopic

sculptures? Has God used anything in your life to teach you a special skill or lesson?

6. Luca says, "There is a God, and that God loves us. That is all we need to know." Andrew needs to believe those words, though he does not realize how much or how soon he will need to believe them—and that they will mean, literally, everything. How do Luca's words play out for Andrew by the end of the story?

7. Lara possesses the trait—some might call it the affliction—of believing that if anything needs accomplishing, she has to acquire the skills for it herself. Do you or anyone you know suffer from that same affliction? What happens if you or they give up control?

8. What do you think Jones means when he says, "Come back with me to Faith's clinic. Let's stop trying to save the world, or even save ourselves. Just help. One person, one at a time. Maybe that's salvation"? How is this a turning point for both Andrew and Lara?